VITO COSTANTINI

Shakespeare: *I am Italian*
He reveals himself in coded messages

Translated from the Italian by Natalia Settembrini Casillas
Edited by Natalia Settembrini Casillas

Youcanprint *Self-Publishing*

Title| Shakespeare: *I am Italian* - He reveals himself in coded messages.

Author | Vito Costantini

ISBN | 978-88-92604-34-6
Graphic Project | Mimma Petarra (Studio Baldari)

Youcanprint Self-Publishing
Via Roma, 73 – 73039 Tricase (LE) – Italy
www.youcanprint.it
info@youcanprint.it
Facebook: facebook.com/youcanprint.it
Twitter: twitter.com/youcanprintit

TABLE OF CONTENTS

Translated from the Italian by Natalia Settembrini Casillas
Edited by Natalia Settembrini Casillas

Natalia Settembrini Casillas was born in Latiano, in the Italian region of Puglia. She came to the United States as a college student and received her degree in psychology from the University of San Francisco, in California. She translated from the Italian the biographical book *One woman, two countries: vignettes of a life fully lived* with the author Evangelina Lisi, and she was the book's editor. Ms. Casillas and her husband Mark, an attorney, live in the beautiful village of Tiburon, overlooking the Golden Gate Bridge, the Bay and the stunning skyline of San Francisco. She is currently writing the story of her family's last two generations, and what it meant growing up as the daughter of a Protestant minister in Catholic Southern Italy after World War II.

Tiburon, California, USA
2016

I

THE BRITISH AND DANTE

If, one day, it would be discovered that Dante were an Englishman, the English people would use any means possible, including political pressure and diplomacy, to make this truth public. And they would not stop until the biography of the author of *The Divine Comedy* would be rewritten, with the official state imprimatur, because of this new fact. Nothing would intimidate them: strong because of their national pride, they would fight to have as their own this greatest of poets. The English people, I am sure, would take Dante back to their country with all the honors due to such poet, and possibly make him their new national icon.

Let's reverse the situation and see how the Italians would act or are acting in a similar situation. Today we have the undeniable truth, and not a simple hypothesis, that Michelangelo and Giovanni Florio, father and son, were the authors of the works penned under the pseudonym William Shakespeare, in particular Giovanni (John for the English) who translated, enlarged and beautified the theatrical works written by his father in the Tuscan language.

The most recent studies confirm this finding, but the Italians, contrary to the British, are a people whose culture is in decline, who disdain their government and consequently have lost hope and pride in anything

Italian, especially their art and culture. The Italians resemble more and more how people of other countries imagine Italians to be, even those who have never visited the peninsula. That is, an indifferent people, concerned only with their daily life, whose love of country disappeared a long time ago. The culture of the 21st Century is found in silly and mindless television shows and not in serious studies, and to take the cause about the identity of Shakespeare is a waste of time because it does nothing to improve their daily life. They are the first in not believing in an *Italian* Shakespeare because they don't believe in themselves. Otherwise, how do you explain and justify the destruction, day after day, of a cultural and artistic patrimony which is the envy of the world? I truly hope that we will change course soon, but I am certainly not holding my breath.

According to the British, the year 2016 will be the four hundredth anniversary of the death of William Shakespeare. In reality, in 1616 died a mediocre actor of Stratford to whom, 7 years later, the English attributed, fraudulently, the works of the two Italians, the Florios, father and son.

It is not necessary to prove my point to examine in depth all the published works of the greatest playwright in history because a few will suffice. Sometimes, the more is published about an author, the less we learn about his life, if this life is based on a lie. In a court of law, the truth can be hidden in two ways: through reticence or through a torrent of words that can be a false truth. All the biographies of Shakespeare, without exception, which begin from the supposition (no longer tolerable) that the illiterate actor is the author of the plays and sonnets known worldwide, are based on false testimony. These biographers are called *Stratfordians*.

The truth is provable in a much easier way than what we have been led to believe, up to now, by the "great" official biographers. A metaphor regarding the formation of the universe may help in understanding what I want to say and will prove in this work: just as the the planets and the stars in the infinite universe were at the beginning a blob of matter that in an explosion became what we know today as our world, so are the publications on Shakespeare, which started with that name in 1623 (the blob of matter exploding in countless books, essays, treatises), which I call the biggest fraud in the literary world. We will start our journey from the present day going back in time, until we arrive at the beginning, the blob of matter, where everything that we need to know will be explained.

In the last four centuries the British have falsified and possibly destroyed documents that would have led to the different and real truth we can prove today. As we have been told and heard many times, there is no perfect crime. Who would have imagined that hidden in commonly used words there are coded messages, and in the phrases seemingly banal or meaningless, information directed to the few able to decipher it? The messages, once decoded, will finally clarify who was behind the name William Shakespeare.[1]

---

[1] These messages remind me of those, seemingly banal and ridiculous, broadcasted during World War II, which were obviously in code, regarding top secret military operations. For example: *The hen has laid an egg*, or *The cow does not give milk*.

As an example, let's use the famous nursery rhyme from the comedy *Love's Labour's Lost*:

> The preyful Princess pierced and pricked a pretty pleasing pricket, some say a sore, but not a sore till now made sore with shooting. The dogs did yell, put L to sore, than sorel jumps from thicket- Or priket sore, or else sorel. The people fall a-hooting . If sore be sore, then "L" to sore makes fifty sores - O sore L! Of one sore I an hundred make, by adding but one more L.[2]

This nursery rhyme, apparently incomprehensible, has an hidden encoded message that only recently has been broken.[3] The *Preyful Princess* is Queen Elizabeth the First, and the killing of the sorel represents, symbolically, Christ's sacrifice, a metaphor for the Eucharist. The letter "L", in fact, denotes the fifty open sores of the Messiah. Through this message Shakespeare was suggesting to the English Queen that she should herself administer directly the sacraments and also become the spiritual head of the Church. A message so strong, regarding the delicate rapport between Church and State, could not be openly told for everybody to see, but only to a few who could understand it and put it into practice.

The age in which Shakespeare lived was full of conspiracies, betrayals and persecutions. An author could openly express his religious and political ideas only within certain limits, and going beyond would be folly, as he risked prison and even death. Only through coded messages could "truths" that were dangerous be expressed. Let's take, as an example, the Catholic Mary,

---

[2] WILLIAM SHAKESPEARE, *Love's Labour's Lost*, 4,2.
[3] GILBERTO SACERDOTI, *Sacrifice and Sovereignty*, Einaudi, 2002

Queen of Scots, who sent a coded message in a conspiracy to dethrone Queen Elizabeth I, and gave her life for this message, after it was decoded.

In this essay eight coded messages, present in the works of Shakespeare, will be decoded. These messages will confirm what is very evident in comparing the official Florio writings with those of the Bard and will help in understanding better the influence of the philospher Giordano Bruno on the author of *Hamlet*.

The final result will be a personal reconstruction of the events no less truthful than the inventions given by the *Stratfordian* biographers.

All of this will be done to give back, ideally, to the Italians, the greatest playwright of all time: the real one, of course.

II

A MAN BORN IN STRATFORD-ON-AVON

In the school books, the encyclopedias and in the many biographies of William Shakespeare, the adverb *probably* recurs constantly: *probably* he attended the local school, *probably* he was a schoolteacher, *probably* he was a horse keeper when he arrived in London, and so forth.[4] Shakespeare's relations with his contemporaries were only relations with a name, not a man. Nobody knew William Shakespeare personally, for the simple reason that the name *Shakespeare*, as we have said, was a stage name. This pseudonym was given later, fraudulently, to the actor of Stratford on Avon who had only the merit of having acted in, or funded, the plays of the real Shakespeare.[5]

Let's stop for a moment and talk about this illiterate man that unfortunately England (and the world) celebrates as the greatest playwright of all time four centuries after his death. Paradoxically, we do not know his exact name. But we know that his birthday, April 23, which strangely coincides with the date of his death (this is also the day on which the British celebrate St. George, patron saint of England), was a posthumous invention. In fact, we must remember that

---

[4] MARK TWAIN, writer and literary critic, in his essay "*Is Shakespeare dead*" talks about the might-have-beeners which we find in the official biographies, all based on conjectures.

[5] Even admitting that the actor of Stratford was ever an actor, he was a minor one, because, having the rural accent of Warwick county, he risked not being understood in London circles, including the Royal Court.

England used the Julian Calendar until 1752, while most of the rest of Europe had started using the Gregorian in 1582. If, regardless of all the doubts, we should believe in his date of birth, for his death we have to calculate 10 extra days, since 11 days were abolished when England decided to be in step with the other countries with the Gregorian Calendar, arriving to May 4. This is one of the most clamorous oversights of whoever devised the most odious and immeasurable fraud in history. What is not an invention is the birthplace of the actor, Stratford on Avon, his marriage to Anne Hathaway, eight years older, the birth of his sons, his work as a grain trader. These are real facts but irrelevant to the person made up by biographers to provide a link to the writing and production of the plays, which is pure invention. There is no evidence, in fact, that he attended the local school, and we know instead that he was born into a family of illiterate people, in a culturally poor village, with a barely elementary, simple everyday education. The father and mother did not know how to write and signed documents and papers with an "x", and his two daughters were unable to read and write. There are only six uncertain and shaky signatures attributed to him and the reason is probably due to a clumsy attempt to falsify the signature of the person who was the real Shakespeare. In the actor's modest last will and testament, also written by a lawyer, there is not a single mention about his activity as a writer, or the least reference to a work or a book in his possession.[6] There are no documents or direct testimonials between him and the principal patrons. He never contributed an introduction, foreword or praise to any literary work of any contemporary author. There is not a contemporary author

---

[6] MARK TWAIN excludes that the man from Stratford knew how to write. His last will and testament was in fact written by a lawyer, Mr. Collins, and the signatures look like ones of a person who knows only how to write his name. And not that well.

who dedicated to him any of his works. He did not leave a library, not even a lonely book. He did not leave a personal letter. The fact that he lived for long periods of time in Stratford should have made him correspond and receive many letters. Moreover, in the immortal plays of Shakespeare, there is never a word about Stratford-on-Avon, but Italy is the focus of many plays. In the 1800s, there were many saboteurs who falsified and trafficked in documents, testimonials and works of Shakespeare. A known forger was Henry Ireland, who fabricated the handwritten play *King Lear* and parts of *Hamlet*. It would be legitimate to think that other people intervened in a dishonest way to create materials useful to a fictitious biography which would tie the man of Stratford to dramas and sonnets not his or to destroy documents compromising for him. In this abominable counterfeiting there is also the funereal monument of the actor, on which there were many changes, including the most clamorous one, in the 1700s, in which a pen and a piece of paper were added to give literary credit to a man without culture, a theatrical impresario who became rich with the theatre, commerce and usury.

III

THE *SHAKESPEARE QUESTION*

The doubts about Shakespeare's identity are not new. The writer Henry James called the divine William "the biggest and most successful fraud ever practiced on a patient world." It is common knowledge that we define *Stratfordians* as those scholars who see in the man born in Stratford-on-Avon the author of the immortal plays. Other interpretations see Edward de Vere, Earl of Oxford, Christopher Marlowe, Francis Bacon and others.

If, for example, it could be established that one of these authors were the real one, of course the national reputation of England would not be damaged: on the contrary, this finding would finally put at rest the *question Shakespeare*. Yet, even though there is proof that the author of the 36 dramas in the First Folio in 1623 was not the man from Stratford, the orthodox critics insist in legitimizing him with arguments that are inconsistent, specious and almost ridiculous, opposing even other British candidates.

This mental closure of the *Stratfordian* academics is, possibly, because, if they opened themselves to a debate, the real author could be found and that could prove that the works of Shakespeare are not English but Italian. According to recent studies by historians who are not involved in British academic circles and the powerful institutions backed by the State, Shakespeare was a man who thought in Italian but wrote in English. It is known that many Italian names in his plays were changed or anglicised with the passing of time. One example is found in the comedy *Measure for Measure*, whose story did not occur in Vienna as it is written, but in

Ferrara.

Again, regarding the play *Two Gentlemen from Verona* it has been demonstrated that Shakespeare chose this city and the northern part of Italy (Milan, Venice and Mantua) because he knew the region very well since he had lived there for long periods of his life.

After all, we don't have to prove over and over that Shakespeare knew Italy, because Italy is everwhere, in every level of his writings: stylistic, linguistic, historic, geographical, topographic, emotional.

IV

A BACKWARD WALK TOWARD THE FLORIOS

Let's clear the air about a common misunderstanding. Many think that regarding Shakespeare only his works should be noted and not if he were English or Italian. It's a rash affirmation, promulgated especially in the world of the theatre, where the actors, busy with the theatrical text, don't care about the biographical data. Nonetheless, Natalino Sapegno, one of the greatest literary critics of the 20th Century, said:

> The works of an author can be fully understood only through an examination of his human and cultural formation and taking into account all that data, including the psychology of his personality... since without the life of the author in its historical position not even the affections and phantasies of the poet would exist, nor his artistic works, or the refraction of the feelings in the poetic works.[7]

The hypothesis that Shakespeare was Italian was advanced for the first time by Santi Paladino, an Italian journalist from Calabria. On February 4, 1927 he published, in a pro-government newspaper, an article in which he argued that the name Shakespeare was the pseudonym of the Italian poet and reformer Michelangelo Florio.[8] Paladino is said to have arrived at this conclusion after finding inside his father's

---

[7] NATALINO SAPEGNO – EMILIO CECCHI, *Italian Literature*, volume VII, page 736, Garzanti Publishing House, 1982.
[8] SANTI PALADINO, in *Impero*, n. 30, February 4, 1927.

extensive and aristocratic library a volume published in 1549 written by the same Florio in which there were sayings and proverbs that about 50 years later would appear in Shakespeare's *Hamlet*.[9] This same journalist, who consequently sustained this hypothesis in an essay, to delve a little deeper into the argument, founded an academy of studies in which many Italian and European scholars participated.[10] The academy was closed a few years later on the authority of the fascist government who accused the journalist (Paladino) of being a Mason. The precious material gathered by the scholars in the academy was confiscated, including the old book of Florio, which was never found. In 1955, after the re-publication of his essay, Paladino said that the real motive of the closure of the Academy had been another, without explaining what it was.[11] Anyway, because of the history of those years, I wonder if the closure of the Academy had occurred to dodge a diplomatic incident. To affirm that the cultural symbol of England could have been Italian would have been extremely offensive for the English. The future Prime Minister Winston Churchill, in that period, was a great supporter of Mussolini and during a visit to Rome, which happened about a month before the publication of the article of Paladino, had praised the politics of *Il Duce*.[12]

During the same years of the journalistic activity of the

---

[9] MICHELANGELO FLORIO, *Second Fruits*, 1549

[10] SANTI PALADINO, *Shakespeare is the pseudonym of an Italian poet?* Reggio Calabria, Borgia, 1929.

[11] SANTI PALADINO, *An Italian author of the Shakesperean plays*, Milano, Gastaldi, 1955.

[12] CHURCHILL TO MUSSOLINI: *"If I were Italian I would have been with you since the beginning: your movement has been of service to the whole world."* And in 1933, exactly when the Academy of Paladino was closed, he told journalists: "Mr. Mussolini is the greatest legislator of the living ones." RICHARD LAMB, *Mussolini and the English*, Corbaccio, 1998, page 108.

Italian journalist from Scilla, Frances Amelia Yates, essayist and British historian, very known and admired in Italian academic circles for her great works on the philosophy of the 1500s and 1600s, especially regarding Giordano Bruno, published an essay on John Florio, son of Michelangelo Florio.[13] Ms. Yates, as I will demonstrate later, discovered the truth about Shakespeare, but decided not to reveal it openly. Referring to a footnote in her book regarding the hypothesis of Paladino, the writer said that there could have been some truth in the words of the journalist.

Beside these above referenced publications, it is interesting to remember an episode regarding the *Encyclopedia Britannica*. The publication in the year 1890 was edited by Thomas Spencer Baynes, one of the most influential British scholars of that time. In this edition, on the entry "Shakespeare", it says that Giovanni (John) Florio, Italian translator, who emigrated to England, was probably the Italian and French languages teacher of Shakespeare when Florio arrived in London around 1590. Baynes arrived at this conclusion after finding many similarities between the translated works of Florio and the plays of the Bard, above and beyond the numerous and detailed references to Italy contained in those plays. In the next edition the *Encyclopedia Britannica*, minus Baynes as its editor, without explanation, any connection between Florio and Shakespeare disappeared.

The books dedicated to the Florios remained for years on the margins of the official culture, perhaps because the two Italians were considered minor authors in the Elizabethan age. Only recently has the academia been speaking about them. Apart from the increasing publications in which it is stated that the actor of Stratford could not have written the plays attributed to him, in 2008 Lamberto Tassinari[14] and

---

[13] FRANCES AMELIA YATES, *John Florio, The Life of an Italian in the England of Shakespeare*, 1934.

[14] LAMBERTO TASSINARI, *Shakespeare? Is the pseudonym of John Florio*, Giano Books, Montreal, 2008.

Saul Gerevini[15] with their respective studies revived the idea that the Florios were the true authors of the dramas signed *William Shakespeare*. Gerevini has also founded, with other scholars, an academy of studies about the Florios.[16] In particular, one of those scholars, Corrado Panzieri, has conducted, for over twenty years, research in the historical archives in Italy and England.

In the year 2012, there was an investigative journalistic story about the Florios on RAI TV, the Italian state official television.[17] In 2013 I authored a historical book written expressely to chronicle the lives of the two Italians out of the academic sphere and to confirm, with research and personal analysis, the truth about the Florios.[18]

---

[15] SAUL GEREVINI, *William Shakespeare, or John Florio: A Florentine to the Conquest of the World,* Pilgrim Editions, Massa Carrara, 2008.
[16] To the Association belong: C. Panzieri, M.O. Nobili, J. Jones, G. Harding. The site is: www.Shakespeareandflorio.net.
[17] ROBERTA ROMANI - IRENE BELLINI, *The Secret of Shakespeare,* Mondadori, Milano, 2012.
[18] VITO COSTANTINI, *Shakespeare is Italian,* Youcanprint, Tricase 2013.

V

A FATHER AND A SON

Michelangelo Florio, called *the Florentine*, was born in Lucca around 1518. He was a Franciscan friar with an encyclopedic knowledge and a great linguistic proficiency. Refined intellectual, he went preaching throughout the whole of Italy under the name of Friar Paolo Antonio.

In 1548 he was caught in the web of the Inquisition and incarcerated in a Roman prison. Here he stayed 27 months, but escaped before his execution. In 1550 he went to London where, once converted to the Evangelical faith, he became an Italian preacher. His culture was such that he was welcomed and immediately feted in aristocratic circles. In a few months he was invited to the court of King Edward VI and soon became tutor to the offspring of the English nobility, including the future Queen Elizabeth. He was particularly attached to the young student Jane Grey who became Queen for only nine days before she was executed.

In this first stay in England an incident stained Michelangelo Florio's reputation because he had an affair with a woman outside of marriage. He risked losing the protection of the powerful William Cecil, Secretary of State, and possibly being sent back to Italy, but he was eventually forgiven. He had a son in 1553, John, with the woman he later married.

The following year, King Edward died and Catholicism returned to England with Mary Tudor.

The preacher was forced to leave the country that had hosted him. He fled with his family to Soglio, a village in Switzerland, where Michelangelo not only continued preaching, but where he also worked as a notary.

In Soglio he wrote several essays,[19] including *Michel Agnolo Fiorentino's Apology* through which we learn some important biographical notes about him. He participated in the debate on The Reformation, renewed his interest in the Italian language and personally devoted himself to the education of his son, John. Once he reached adolescence, John studied at the University of Tübingen and then at various Italian universities, but he did not graduate.

With the rise of Elizabeth I in England, father and son returned to London. Here Michelangelo remained under wraps, for fear of being re-taken by the Inquisitors, devoting himself entirely to writing. John became a tutor and worked as a translator and lawyer in the French Embassy, where he became friendly with Giordano Bruno, a guest in the same embassy from 1583 to 1585.

John published *First fruits* in 1578, a bilingual manual of Italian-English languages, accompanied by an Italian grammar. He also translated several Italian works.

Two years later he married Rose Daniel, sister of the poet Samuel Daniel and in 1584 he published a compendium of poetry, *Pandora*, under the pseudonym of John Soowthern.[20]

Subsequently, the translator became a friend of well-known and prestigious intellectuals, such as Philip Sidney, poet and courtier, author of the novel *Arcadia*, which Florio read and opined on. Sidney introduced the Italian to an exclusive club, the *School of night*, whose members, some of the greatest exponents of English culture, were interested in giving answers on the more hidden aspects of human existence. In 1591 John published another manual, *Second fruits* with an appendix in which he added about 6,000 Italian proverbs

---

[19] *Apologia of M. Agnolo Fiorentino (1557); Works of Giorgio Agricola of the art of metals (1563); History of the life and death of the illustrious Giovanna Graia (1607); Regulations and institutions of the Tuscan language (manuscript).*
[20] Hypothesis of LAMBERTO TASSINARI.

collected by his father Michelangelo in Italy. Beginning with this publication, John added the prefix *Resolute* to his name. From this day on he will sign his works *Resolute John Florio*.

Soon after this decision, there appeared for the first time in the London theater the dramas of Shakespeare.

There is some evidence that during that time, for a while, John Florio was also a secret agent in the service of the powerful Francis Walsingham, head of the English Secret Service. This would explain the knowledge of the dynamics of political plots and super-plots in the works of Shakespeare/Florio.

In 1598 Florio published *A world of words*, the first, authentic modern Italian-English dictionary, which he began around 1590, an extraordinary work for its wealth of terms, more than 46,000 Italian words, 74,000 in the reprint and 150,000 English words. John Florio wanted his dictionary to be used by everyone, but especially by scholars, so they could read works that in England were unavailable to the people who could not read Italian, in particular to read Dante, Petrarch, and Boccaccio. From recent studies it has come to light that whoever needs clarifications on the language of Shakespeare must refer necessarily to this dictionary, in which you can see the grammatical technique through which the great playwright would forge new words, ideas, thoughts. These linguistic techniques had already been used in the works of Florio before the actor from Stratford ever appeared and the dramas of Shakespeare were staged (but today we know that Florio and Shakespeare were one and the same). To compile this dictionary, Florio read more than 250 books, some of which served Shakespeare (Florio) as sources for composing dramas.

Simultaneously, while writing and preparing his dictionary, John worked on the translation of the *Essays of Montaigne*, published in English in 1603, probably one of the most influential books ever published in England. These translations became very fashionable and were read over and over for years and generations. Its contribution in understanding the literary development of Shakespeare/Florio is very relevant, if you think that some of the dramas, as *The Tempest,* are extensively modeled on the *Essays* translated by the same Florio.

Michelangelo Florio died in 1605. John continued his social ascendancy, and with the accession to the throne of James I, John became tutor to the children of the King, and Queen Anne's secretary. As a sign of the esteem he had for James I, John Florio translated into Italian the sovereign's writing, *Basilikon Doron* (Royal Gift) that became important to many works of Shakespeare.

In 1612 the sudden death of Prince Henry, who would have been the future king of England, caused John incredible sorrow. Seven years later, in 1619, with Queen Anne's death, Florio was exiled from the court.

In the last years of his life John translated into English the stories of Boccaccio and put together the *First Folio,* where he gathered all his works, signed *William Shakespeare.* Afterwards, he retired to Fulham, on the outskirts of London, where he remained until he died of the plague in 1625.

John Florio's last will and testament, written in the year of his death, reveals an incredible affinity and similarity to the writings and thinking of Shakespeare. It has been shown that in the Bard's plays there appears Dante's language and a deep knowledge of the *Divine Comedy.*[21] At the time of the composition of the works signed *Shakespeare,* only John Florio had such knowledge in England: the first complete translation of Dante in the English language will not appear for two more centuries.[22]

---

[21] FRANK KERMODE, *The language of Shakespeare,* Bompiani, 2000.
[22] *The Divine Comedy,* which was completely translated into English only in 1802, would have been inaccessible to a Shakespeare who spoke little or no Italian. Florio owned four editions of the *Comedy.*

VI

COMPARING TWO PASSAGES

Michelagelo Florio, as I have related from his biography, in his first stay in England, was also the tutor of Jane Grey. To her, years later, he dedicated a book where, in a passage, he reports the reaction of his young pupil to the recounting of the months spent in prison by the young Franciscan monk. Here are the words of Michelango:

> I, myself, in telling her one day of the **outrages**, the **scorns** and the tortures that I suffered in Rome in the space of twenty-seven months, because I preached in Naples, Padua and Venice the true religion of Christ, I saw her crying and, raising her eyes to the sky, she said "God, please, do not let in so much suffering for all your children in this world."[23]

Now, let's see what is is written in the drama *Othello* when the protagonist of the tragedy narrates his past to Desdemona:

> I had from her the fervent prayer to recount fully the history of my adventures of which she had heard only a part, and never all at once. I agreed and often I extracted tears when I spoke of the misfortunes suffered in my youth. When I finished, she paid me back with a world of sighs.[24]

The episode of two young women who are moved to tears on hearing the tales of two men is not a simple coincidence.

---

[23] MICHELANGELO FLORIO, *History of the life and death of Lady Jane Grey.*
[24] *Othello*, 1, 3.

Michelangelo used a real episode in his life to create the scene between Othello and Desdemona. I want to emphasize also that I can find many analogies of this type when comparing the works of the Florios and the dramas of Shakespeare. But if there are any doubts left on the passages just read, observe the two words **outrages** and **scorns** that Michelangelo chose to describe his suffering in the Roman prison because they re-appear in the famous monologue of *Hamlet* when the prince of Denmark speaks about *the scorns of time* and *outrageous fortune.*[25]

As I have mentioned in the previous chapter, with the ascension to the throne of the Catholic Mary Tudor in 1554, the Florios left England and went to live in Soglio, Switzerland. Here John received his first teachings from his father who, being also passionate about the theater, wrote plays in the Tuscan language, left for a time in the drawer. He continued writing dramas until the death of his wife and his return to London in 1577 to be with John. John had gone back to England a few years before.

Michelangelo decided to go back to England, where he felt safe, because the Inquisition was still in existence in Europe, but also to help introduce his son to the aristocratic world. As time went by, being in the company of the rich and noble, proved to be quite expensive and so John decided to translate (and not only translate, but enlarge and beautify) the dramas written by his father so they could be produced and make some money, a choice that he made definitively by putting before his name, starting in 1591, the adjective *Resolute*, a mark of solemn commitment to himself to never turn back from that decision. But, let's note that the words *Resolute John Florio* appear only in the translated works, not in the dramas, which were still anonymous.

---

[25] It was MASSIMO O. NOBILI who pointed out that the words *Scorn* (clearly imported from Italy and little known in England, probably only by the Florios) and *outrageous* (which becomes an adjective) are found in the famous monologue of Hamlet.

Choosing anonymity had a motive: the English did not tolerate that a foreigner could publish poetry or dramas in the English language, but only translations. According to John Florio the English had *a knife ready to slit my throat* if he had done it.[26]

The adjective *Resolute* was heavy with meaning for the Italian translator. At this time, together with this choice of name, there appeared on the London theatrical scene some plays whose greatness was immediately manifest and only later were they associated with the name *Shakespeare*. These plays were firstly staged by the troupe of Richard Burbage, actor and producer, and then later, with an associate of his, a young illiterate country actor from Stratford, then also producer, with a good head for business, the same actor who, 30 years later will be deified by the British as a genius, incredibly cultured man and the greatest, most admired and most celebrated playwright in the history of the world.

---

[26] Introduction to the Dictionary *A World of Words.*

VII

THE PEN NAME

At the end of 1592 the theaters closed because of the plague. In 1593 in the published poem *Venus and Adonis* we see for the first time the name of an unknown author, William Shakespeare, and the following year, by the same author, *The Rape of Lucretia*. As was said at the beginning of this essay, Shakespeare is the stage name of the Florios, and it has nothing to do with the Sicilian name *Crollalanza*, belonging to a noble woman of that region, which literally translates into *Shakespeare*, like some critics, but only a few, have speculated.

Before we find the motive behind this choice of name, it is necessary to provide an explanation. In the Elizabethan era, playrights and actors were not considered literary people or artists, but on the same level as the agents of the actors and the proprietors of the theater, and as the owners and operators of circuses and bordellos. The authors who made their living from the theatre could be, at the same time, co-owners of the building and usually had an oral or written contract with the producers. It is understood that in this situation the criterion for choosing a play was not because of its literary brilliance, but for its commercial potential. Once the play was sold, the author lost every right and the play became property of the company which had acquired it. The company, then, could do anything it wanted with it. The job of the playright was pretty remunerative, he made more money than a teacher or preacher, but the reputation for anyone who worked in the theater was one of the lowest and most of the them would do anything possible not to have their name associated with that world.

The biographers of the Bard emphasize two unusual things about him. The first is this: the plays penned with the name *Shakespeare* were always produced, since 1594, from its date of inception, by the company *Lord Chamberlain's Men*, later called *King's Men*. This faithfulness is not found with any other author. The second one is that the plays were never given in person by Shakespeare to the printers, who, obviously, could not make any changes, contrary to what had happened with the two little poems we have cited, which were impeccably prepared for printing.

In reality, these strange facts can be easily explained if we decide that behind the person with the name Shakespeare are the Florios, hiding in his shadow. Let's begin in 1593, when the name *Shakespeare* appears for the first time, exactly in the year that the plague resumed. In those times, there was a heated xenophobia and the authorities were busy trying to contain episodes of violence against any foreigner. John Florio was a foreigner and his father was wanted by the Italian inquisition. This fact alone can explain why the Florios always used the same company, because giving the plays to different companies would have multiplied the danger of losing their anonymity. For the same reason, except for the two initial poems, they never gave any play personally to the printer and they lost interest in them after they were sold to the company.

What I just said about the attitude of the Florios seems inconceivable if we put the plays as being written by the actor from Stratford. This man, able tradesman and usurer, would never have left the plays so readily before obtaining all he could to the last penny, till there was only a bone left, and no flesh.

Returning to the Florios, it is easily understood why publishing the two poems under their Italian name would have been folly, and this was also applicable to the plays that they had put in circulation in the London market. But John, the *Resolute*, is the only one who, since his father Michelangelo, an old man and terrified of the Inquisition, and finally outside the social and cultural life, at a certain time decided to put an end to their complete anonymity. It was then, following the method of his friend Giordano Bruno,[27] that John found a pseudonym that would reflect, in hermetic form, the origin, culture and the objectives that the Florios wanted to achieve, that is to bring to England the Italian culture and elevate the English language, at the time the least admired of the European languages. The pseudonym *William Shakespeare* was perfect in that sense. That it was a pseudonym is easy to demonstrate because we find in the documents in London of the time that no man existed with that name. It was exactly with that name that the Florios launched their most important encoded message.

---

[27] G. BRUNO, *The Shadows of the Ideas*. Bruno writes: "To those who will be permitted to learn the most profound principles of art ... remember not to divulge them to everyone without discretion." The man from Nola had great influence on Shakespeare/Florio.

VIII

FIRST ENCODED MESSAGE
Shake-Speares

Let's put our magnifying glass on the pseudonym *William Shakespeare*, starting with the name **William**, a very common name in England. If we separate the letters of the name in a certain way we have **Will I am**, and if the words are moved around we have the phrase **I am Will**. So, when we read "I am will", which in English means willingness, resolution, in this way, John wanted to replicate the adjective **resolute** that he put before his signature in his translation works (**Resolute** John Florio). Using the name William, he created a hermetic and ideal bridge to connect the translations he could do, which were permitted to foreigners in England, with the poetic and theatrical plays, which were forbidden to those same foreigners.

Now let's examine the surname Shakespeare. John, as his father, was incredibly versed in and a great expert of classical culture, and he searched in mythology for an appropriate stage name. He found inspiration in Athena, the goddess who in myth holds and shakes a spear, and according to John Florio, symbolically, similar to a pen shaken against ignorance. But not everyone knows that the pseudonym *William Shakespeare*, which first appeared in the two poems, was later replaced with Shake-Speares, two separate names. It has also been noted that in 15 of the 33 dramas published before the *First Folio* in 1623 the name of the playwright was written that way, a characteristic without precedents in the world of literature. It would be quite interesting to understand why Florio at this time in his life decided not to

29

use the pseudonym of before, but with the name separated by a dash in two.

I do not believe that the transformation was attributable to esthetics, because, as we have seen so far, behind every choice that the Italian made there was a hidden motive. Let's see what that is in this instance.

Around 1590 or so, despite John's cautious behavior, his name began to circulate in theatrical circles, although nobody was sure if he was the author or the editor of the dramas performed. At the same time, he was also accused by his detractors, who could not explain his literary prolificacy, of plagiarizing the works of other writers. For this reason the Italian wanted to emphasize, with an encrypted message, that such wealth of literary and theatrical production was not explainable by plagiarism, but because, with him, there was another writer, his father, a collaborator of sort in his plays.

Let's examine the name **Shake-Speares**: these are two names linked by a hyphen, with the final 's', in the English language denoting the plural, because the Florios were two, different persons but with the same last name and part of the same family. It is a pseudonym chosen by the Florios to symbolize Michelangelo-John, father and son, a stage name, as we said, suggested by the myth of the birth of Athena, coming out from the head of Zeus, already adult and brandishing a spear. The meaning is as follows: Michelangelo (**Shake**) writes dramas (or sketches them or provides useful material for their development) and in that way shakes the mind of John (**Speare**), who translates, expands them, embellishes with his pen (spear). John, like Athena, came out from the head of the parent in the sense that the culture of the parent was transmitted to the son.[28]

---

[28] In the *First Folio* of 1623, and Michelangelo dead, John Florio started re-using (and signing) the name *Shakespeares*. Later on, the English will delete also the final 's', plural, meaning the two Florios, in a process of gradual concealment.

But all of this is still not enough to explain the choice of the myth, because there is another, stronger motivation. To find this other motive, let's find the origin of the name of the goddess on the Italian encyclopedia Treccani:

> The goddess Athena is designated in two ways: simply as Athena or as Pallade Athena; two names, these last two, who are never shown separated in the writings of Homer or Hesiod. It is attributed by most to the first (Pallade) a predicative value, speaking of **the strength that moves the spear**; in the root of the second there is hidden the idea of **blooming youth**.

The Florios were great scholars of the Greek civilization, and therefore they knew very well what the name Athena meant. Its verbal root is connected to flower. As the name makes reference mainly to flower and flowering, we understand why the Italian chose it. The name Florio, in fact, derives from flower. Under the portrait of John, the only one that has reached us, are printed the following Latin verses, translated here:

> Content with his own worth, noble in his art, Italian in tongue, English at heart, both at once in his work/ he **flourished** still and **will flourish** in the future./ He who loves him desires that **Florio, florid** in this portrait, may continue **to flourish**.

Along with these words there appears the image of the sunflower, a flower that for its characteristics is well suited for the symbolic meaning of two different entities, since a part of it is constantly illuminated, while the other lives in shadow, a situation in which the Florios found themselves in relation to their plays.

At the conclusion of our discussion we have to understand, choosing that pseudonym, what role was played by the actor-businessman of Stratford. This man had arrived in London just a little bit earlier than the time in which John chose his pseudonym, and becoming part of the same company to which the Italian had given some of his plays, already produced, anonymously.

The name of the actor, according to official documents, varies from time to time. Sometimes it is **Will Shaksper**, sometimes **Saxsper** or **Shasber**. Some historians affirm that the similarity of these names with the pseudonym *William Shakespeare* of the Florios created the *quid pro quo*, the misunderstanding and the identity swap which has resulted in the biggest literary fraud in history.

I want to explore two hypotheses. The first, if truly the actor was named with one of the three names above, that name could have suggested to John Florio, a wizard with words, his *William Shakespeare*, a pseudonym containing those messages which we already analyzed and also similar to the name of the actor just arrived in London. In this case, the misunderstanding would have been created *ad hoc* by John to solidify his anonymity, because the ambiguity would have created uncertainty. Moreover, by choosing as an alter ego the name of a man, so ignorant, uncouth and coarse, would have permitted the Florios, if the attitude of the English might change later on, to take back their paternity of the plays without any recrimination from the name-lender of Stratford. The second hypothesis is that, since we don't know even now the real name of the actor, the three above names could represent a clumsy attempt by the actor himself, after the successes of the plays, to record the name for himself in the official documents of the time (scarcely controlled by the officials, who oftentimes were also corruptible), with the pseudonym of the Florios. It's not difficult to entertain the notion that, in the course of hundreds of years, with the endgame being the transformation of an illiterate actor into the most celebrated playright of all time, the English might have tampered with legal documents, parish documents and even creating a false genealogy.[29]

---

[29] In the matrimonial documents of November 27, 1582 saved in Worcester you can read *Wm Shaxpere*. The day after becomes *William Shagspere*. The documents were written many times in a clumsy manner.

Of course, the certainty of the identity Florio-Shakespeare, I repeat, is not based only on the interpretation of the encoded messages left by John Florio, but by comparing the official writings of the two Italians and those of Shakespeare (that is, their own writings).

IX

THE UPSTART CROW

The dramas of the Florios, staged by the company of the *Lord Chamberlain's Men*, become very successful. The two Italians receive a percentage of the proceeds but, even though the plays were anonymous, the intellectuals and the aristocrats know that the author is the Italian translator John Florio. In a famous Robert Greene quote taken from a pamphlet published in 1593, which evidently escaped from the web of lies that do not want the Florios to be the real authors of the dramas and sonnets, perpetrated for centuries against them, it clearly speaks of John as the author of Shakespeare's plays.[30] This citation was published after the representation of *Henry VI*, in which a feminine personage is defined, because of her aggressive behavior, *heart of a tiger hidden under the skin of a woman*. Greene is an intellectual, with master's degrees from Cambridge and Oxford, of a sour disposition, envious of John Florio who, even though he does not have a degree, has a lot of success in writing translated works, especially theatrical plays.

The sentence is this:

> There is an upstart **crow**, beautified with our feathers, that with his **tiger's heart wrapt in a player's hide**, supposes he is as well able to bombast out a blank-verse as the best of you: and being an absolute **Johannes** factotum, is in his own conceit the only Shakescene in a country.[31]

---

[30] It has been demonstrated by Saul Gerevini (who, by the way, thinks that Thomas Nashe is the real author of the libel) in a study that I mention now only so I can connect it to what I will speak about later on.

[31] ROBERT GREENE, *A Groatsworth of Wit*, 1593.

Greene could not express himself more clearly because he was afraid to be denounced, but in that period everyone knew he was talking about John Florio. This quote appears today in the encyclopedias, in the textbooks and in any writing dedicated to the Bard because in it, for the first time, we find the name *Shakespeare* near some dramas initially anonymous: Scholars explain that the adjective *Shakescene* is the playwright's name. *Shakescene*, at that time, **defined a bad actor or playright, a mummer, whose only contribution to the theater was the shaking of the planks as he walked on the stage.** For this reason, Greene, furiously, substitutes the name Shakespeare with *Shakescene* for assonance, a practice widely used in English poetry. Here it ends the interpretation of the English, willingly ignoring the rest, much more important than the premise. Let's then see the rest. The *upstart crow*, as I will fully demonstrate in the next pages, is undoubtedly the *careerist*, the *parvenu* John Florio, who writes one drama after another and quickly (also because, as we know today, he translated the many writings of his father Michelangelo). John, as we have said, is accused by Greene, who cannot explain the literary fertility of the Italian translator, of copying from other writers' works, of scholars, in a way to exalt himself. Greene surely does not speak about the actor of Stratford on Avon, but certainly of John, *Henry VI's* true author. John Florio is defined (using the words in that drama in a parody meant to belittle him) as *heart of a tiger hidden in the skin of an actor*, in the sense that the author John, in a cowardly way, hides behind an actor. That the author is the Italian translator is obvious, because in the quote there is even his Latinized name, *Johannes* (John) and the adjective *factotum*, Florio's nickname, as the Italian himself informs us in his dictionary.[32] Let's observe in the

---

[32] Florio writes that it was Hugh Sanford, secretary to the noble family of the Pembrokes, who first coined the name for him. Sanford may have had the idea from the book *Second Fruits* by Florio, in which the Italian was

quote also the adjective *absolute* that Greene does not put in by chance: it is an ironic reference and for assonance (as he does with *Shakescene*) to the adjective *resolute* that John Florio put before his name in his translation works.

---

reprising citations of classical authors on love seen as the owner of the world. Florio writes that Cupid had taken "from Mars his sword, from Neptune his trident and from Jupiter his bolt of lightning, and from Homer his verses and from Hercules his club. So, as a dictator is Dominus **Factotum**, who is if not him?" Using the definition factotum to describe Florio, Sanford wanted to convey the idea (just as Greene did) that Florio took, and plagiarized plays of others, just as Eros had taken from Mars the sword, from Neptune the trident, etc.

X

SECOND ENCODED MESSAGE
Twelve years in prison

After Michelangelo Florio's death in 1605, John Florio continued translating his father's last dramas. The actor, of whom we still don't know the exact written form of his name, after enriching himself with the works of the two Italians, retired around that time to Stratford-on-Avon to become a grain trader, buying properties and completely ceased any activity in London.

The company *Lord Chamberlain's Men*, meanwhile, had changed its name to *King's Men* and was under the tutelage of James I, the successor to Queen Elizabeth. As I have already said, John Florio had a high position at court and around 1609 wrote that strange comedy, *The Tempest*, that according to the scholars is completely different from the other comedies. It is so for two reasons: first, because it was written only by John without the help of his father who had died, secondly, because it is an autobiographical work in allegorical form and is the story of the life of the Florios.[33]

In *Shakespeare is Italian* I wrote an entire chapter to demonstrate it. Here, instead, I will limit myself to extrapolate from the play a phrase which contains a similar meaning to another just examined (*heart of a tiger hidden in the skin of an actor*), only to add another piece in the reconstruction of the identity of Shakespeare. The play is about a father and daughter on a deserted island.[34] It has been

---

[33] L. TASSINARI speaks about the allegoric content of the comedy, without delving in.

[34] CORRADO PANZIERI asserts that Shakespeare (Florio) in describing the

37

said, and I agree, that Prospero represents Michelangelo Florio, while his daughter Miranda represents John. The savage island on which the two land is England.[35] In the play it is written that Prospero, having learned the magician's arts on the island, frees from the hollow of a tree the air's spirit Ariel, personification of the imagination. The spirit was imprisoned for 12 years by a witch. It is written:

> She did confine thee, by help of her more potent ministers and in her most unmitigable rage, into a cloven pine, within which rift imprisoned thou didst painfully **remain a dozen years.**[36]

We know that the name Shakespeare appeared for the first time in *Venus and Adonis* in 1593 and that Michelangelo Florio died in 1605. John chose the imprisonment of the spirit and the number 12 for a reason. He wanted to emphasize the 12 years during which the dramas of the Florios were entrusted to a theatrical company. That choice caused them pain since they were unable to reveal that they were the plays' real authors. In other words, the imagination was imprisoned in the body of the actor who recited the tragedies of the Florios: in the drama's metaphor the actor is the cavity of the tree, in which is hidden the imagination of the Florios.

---

place used the island of Vulcan. A truly remote spot for the actor from Stratford, but not for Michelangelo Florio.

[35] John Florio wants to say, metaphorically, that England is a savage place linguistically and culturally compared to Italy.

[36] The Tempest, 1.2

XI

SONNETS AND HOMOSEXUALITY

For centuries the English biographers, trying to attribute at all costs the Sonnets to that actor from Stratford on Avon, have had to deal with the homosexuality of their author. This has created some embarrassment, because if on one hand with such stupendous lyrics the scholars want to put into evidence the poetic grandeur of the Bard, on the other they could not stomach, for manly pride, that the same were directed to a man. Consequently, they thought to resolve the problem by minimizing this aspect of the personality of the poet, or, as some have done, transforming the playright into a playboy, the perfect lover of the English noble women. If, instead, we put back the pieces in their rightful place, and put aside the prejudice, all becomes easier.

To solve the mystery of these poems, we have to give a last look at Michelangelo Florio's biography. As noted above, he escaped from prison in Rome shortly before his execution, and in 1550 took refuge in London. Here he was appointed as the Evangelist preacher in the Italian community, but then he had an affair with the woman whom he later married and who gave him a son, John.

This love affair in our view was "planned" by the preacher, for he wanted to divert the attention of the community and especially of his patron William Cecil, from a story much more serious and dangerous, ready to explode and become public knowledge. Michelangelo, thirty-four at the time, had fallen into a homosexual relationship with his pupil Henry Herbert, son of the Earl of Pembroke. Henry was, at 16, a very beautiful and feminine boy to whom Michelangelo was teaching the Tuscan language.

Michelangelo dedicated to Henry some sonnets written in Tuscan, later translated by John into English. The same John added other sonnets dedicated to his future wife Rose (*the dark lady*),[37] sister of his close friend and poet Samuel Daniel. John wrote the lyrics when the woman seemed indifferent to his advances and more inclined to accept those of Thomas Nashe, the so-called rival poet.[38]

For centuries the young man for whom the lyrics were written was unknown, and whose name, as I will demonstrate, is that of Henry Herbert, the son of the Earl of Pembroke.

During all of his life, Michelangelo nurtured a deep feeling of love for his student who later married Mary Sidney (sister of Philip Sydney), poetess, woman of great culture, and translator. We have evidence of the love affair between teacher and student: Michelangelo, before he died, entrusted his son John to give the 340 precious volumes of the Florios' library to William Herbert, son of Henry Herbert, who had died four years earlier.

Our conclusions arise not only from the bequest, but by their behavior toward each other over the years. It is true that for the sonnets, as with the dramas, any written testimony that could prove the authorship of the Florios has been destroyed, but, as in other cases, there are coded messages that will help us.

---

[37] JONATHAN BATE, *The genius of Shakespeare*, Oxford University Press, 1998. The mysterious *dark lady* according to Bate is Rose. In the sonnet CIX her name shows up.
[38] Hypothesis of SAUL GEREVINI on the identity of the rival poet.

XII

THIRD ENCODED MESSAGE
The enigmatic dedication

The sonnets were published by Thomas Thorpe in 1609. In the introduction they have the following enigmatic dedication written by Thorpe himself, here reported as it appears in the original text.

TO. THE. ONLIE.
BEGETTER. OF. THESE.
INSUING. SONNETS. **Mr.**
W.H. ALL. HAPPINESSE.
AND. THAT.
ETERNITIE.
PROMISED.
BY.
OVR. EVER-LIVING.
POET. WISHETH.
THE. WELL-
WISHING.
ADVENTVRER. IN.
SETTING.
FORTH.
- T.T.

(To the only inspirer of the following sonnets, Mr. W. H., every happiness and the eternal promise from our immortal poet wishes the best who wishing the best ventures into publishing. T. T.)

The key to understanding this dedication is the word *begetter*, whose meaning is *procreator*, even though the majority of scholars say that it should be explained as

41

inspirer. It looks like a detail to be overlooked, but it is not.

According to this interpretation, the initials W. H. refer to **William Herbert** (son of Henry, the young man whom I think was the lover of Michelangelo Florio), or, changing the place of the letters, **Henry Wriothesley**, Earl of Southampton, protector, according to English academics, of the actor who came from Stratford on Avon. In other words, the poet Shakespeare would have been inspired by one of the two noblemen, with whom he would have had an overwhelming and at the same time very tender homosexual passion.

It needs to be said, incidentally, that there are no documents that would prove any ties between the actor and the two noblemen, while we know there is a bond between the noblemen and John Florio, the real Shakespeare, because the Italian had been the tutor of Henry Wriothesely from 1585 to 1590.

The thesis that behind these mysterious initials there is one of the two noblemen is not possible according to some historians, because the letters are preceded by **Mr.**, which at that time meant Master, title meaning economic independence of the person who has that title, but not belonging to a noble family. For others, the term *begetter* means *procurer*. In this case the dedication of the printer Thorpe was for the unknown person who had given him the manuscript of the sonnets, a thesis also without foundation because it contrasts with the wish of eternity inside the dedication: this cannot be done to a man just because he gave him some lyrics which, anyway, were already circulating in literary circles for a few years.

Let's pause a moment, and let's see how the sonnets appear from a formal point.

It has been shown that Shakespeare (we say Florio) did not intervene in their publication because if it could have been possible to influence in any way the printing, this would have been more correct as in the two early poems *Venus and Adonis* and *The Rape of Lucretia*.

Shakespeare, moreover, would not have agreed to add to

the lyrical compendium the little poem *A Lover's Complaint*, whose worth is sharply lower than the *Sonnets*, almost as if it belonged to another author, besides being evidently incomplete. And there was no reason to publish it before polishing it and finishing it, because, as many scholars say, Shakespeare, the actor from Stratford, had still seven more years to live (but, since I think that Florio was the real Shakespeare, sixteen more).

So then, excluding the two noblemen and an eventual unknown *procurer* of the sonnets, *who is this mysterious W. H.?* Before answering, it is quite interesting to read the information given by the aforementioned British scholar Frances Amelia Yates, author of the most complete and important biography of John Florio dated 1934, when access to determined documents was paradoxically easier than it is today:

> In 1609, Thorpe addressed to William Herbert, Earl of Pembroke – via Florio – a translated satire and to "Mr. W. H." a sonnets-sequence by William Shakespeare.[39]

Following this information, some biographers argue that Florio was given the task by his friend the printer Thomas Thorpe to give two plays to William Herbert. In reality, if we pay attention, it is written that Florio gave William Herbert the translation of a satire[40] and W. H. the *Sonnets* of Shakespeare, as if they were two different persons, otherwise Ms. Yates would have simply written only that Florio gave the satire and the sonnets of Shakespeare to William Herbert, without adding anything more.

The historian (Yates) had a valid motive to write in such a way. As I said, she wrote almost *sotto voce*, in a marginal note in her book, in order not to exclude that (in the words of

---

[39] F. A. YATES, *John Florio,* op. cit. p. 291.

[40] JOHN HEALEY, *Discovery of a new world*.

the journalist Santi Paladino) there could be some truth regarding the hypothesis that the Bard could be Italian. Ms. Yates, great expert of the hermetic tradition and of Giordano Bruno, probably succeeded in decyphering the contents of the dedication of the sonnets and to whom the mysterious initials belonged. The phrase, in fact, is a type of *lapsus* revealing the certitude of Ms. Yates (even though she never said so openly) that behind the name *Shakespeare* there were the Florios. And we should not deviate from her affirmation that Florio gave to W. H. the sonnets of *Shakespeare*, because we could also understand that John Florio gave W. H. his own sonnets and those of his father signed *Shakespeare*, the pen name the two Italians had chosen.

Ms. Yates knew that in those initials was the *Question Shakespeare*, but she preferred to keep silent, even though she made clear, using a formal stratagem, that surely W. H. was not William Herbert nor Henry Wriothesley, of whom she would have had no problem writing the first and last name clearly.

This explains why, while referring to the addressee of the satire, the historian Yates wrote the nobleman's name in its entirety (William Herbert), but regarding the sonnets she preferred leaving the initials W.H. without specifying to whom they belonged, contributing in perpetuating the mystery of Shakespeare and with her silence, another accomplice, in my opinion, to the biggest fraud of the literary world.

So, what did the historian uncover?

We begin by saying that the publication of the sonnets, long circulating in manuscript, and the unpublished poem *A Lover's Complaint* in possession of the Pembrokes, was requested by that family, especially by Mary Sidney. The countess excluded from the beginning any participation of John Florio, both in the editing and in the printing. However, the printer Thorpe, friend of the Italian translator, asked Florio to write the dedication, which Thorpe then signed. Thorpe did it because he knew the truth about the sonnets and their authors. The dedication is therefore a kind of ownership and paternity of the sonnets, in an encrypted seal that the Italian wanted to impart to his words and those of his father and that here we want to decode.

Let's go back to the term *begetter* that in some Italian translations is sometimes *ispiratore* (inspirer) or *procuratore* (procurer), often also used by English historians.

In reality, as I have said previously, it means *procreator*, *father*, and in a figurative sense, *author*.[41] If we understand the term correctly the meaning of the dedication changes completely because W. H. becomes the author of the sonnets and not the inspirer or the procurer. But since the author of the sonnets is William Shakespeare, the initials should be W. S.

But something is wrong. Look carefully at the dedication, as it was written in the press in 1609: every word is followed by a full stop, in all 30. Even the sum of the letters that compose the names of Michelangelo Florio and Henry Herbert, the two lovers, is 30: to each full stop corresponds a letter. Following a hermetic praxis of the sixteenth century, we believe that behind the initials W. H. is hidden not one author, but two, united in one person. This for two reasons: because they are the lovers *procreators* of the lyrics (author and addressee) and because they are the authors of two different compositions (sonnets and poem). In the book printed by Thorpe these initials have been turned upside down. According to the handwriting of classic Latin, the **W** is **M** turned upside down, initial of **M**ichelangelo, while the **H**, which even turned upside remains the same, is the initial of the name **H**enry: in this way, symbolically, we go from appearance to reality and vice versa. The first letter refers to Michelangelo, the name of teacher, tutor, magister, as the title Mr. prefixed to the name was understood at the time of

---

[41] RINA SARA VIRGILLITO translates with *procreator* in Shakespeare - *The Sonnets*, GTE Newton, 1988, p. 9.

publication. The second letter refers to the name of a noble (Henry Herbert Pembroke) the title of whom is implicit in the family of origin.

In light of these considerations, we can understand why John Florio used the term *begetter* in the dedication: for the double meaning of author and father.[42]

The Sonnets, in fact, had been written by his father, even though John had translated and amplified them.

In this sense, the adjective *onlie* could also be understood not necessarily as *the only one*, but, as some people have said, as *the principal*, meaning Michelangelo Florio, who was the main author of the sonnets.

But we have more. John chose to precede Mr. to the name of his father because *Magister* was the title that Michelangelo had used in his writings published in Italy.[43]

Considering all of these facts, the dedication should thus be interpreted this way:

> To the principal author of these sonnets, Magister Michelangelo Florio (and Henry Herbert: author and recipient intended as only one person) every happiness and that eternity promised by our immortal poet (Michelangelo himself) wishes who (Thorpe) with good wishes embarks in the adventure of publication T. T.

John Florio hid himself behind Thorpe's signing and wished for his father and Henry Herbert, both deceased, eternal happiness and eternity in the memory of men, the same as Michelangelo had promised to his student and lover with the sonnets.

The phrase of Ms. Yates has now a new meaning:

---

[42] To beget: to procreate as the father. In the Bible: 'Mehujael begat Methusael and Methusael begat Lamech' – Gen. 4:18.

[43] The title M. (magister) appears, for example, in the Apology of **M.** Michel Angelo Fiorentino and in *Historia*, of **M.** Michelangelo Florio Fiorentino.

Thorpe sent William Herbert, through Florio, the translation of a satire and the sonnets of Shakespeare created by W. H. (M. Florio and H. Herbert).

It is important to know that John Florio was on good terms with William Herbert and his brother Philip, but not so with their mother, Mary Sidney Pembroke, Henry's widow. She always had a formally friendly attitude towards the Florios, but hostile in essence. This not only for the ancient love affair between Michelangelo and her husband, but also because, herself a poetess, she could not stand that an Italian had produced such great lyrics, masterfully translated by another Italian who had even expanded the collection. This was the woman's feeling towards the Florios: it is evident by the following emblematic episode. In 1590 John edited the novel *Arcadia* of Philip Sidney, Mary's brother, who had died in 1586 fighting in the Netherlands. When the sonnets began to circulate in manuscript, Mary Sidney, even though there was no need, had the work revised by her secretary Hugh Sanford, replacing the excellent work done by John with a much inferior version published in 1593.

She was still hostile toward the Florios when, in 1609, she requested the printing of the sonnets and the poem *The Lover's Complaint*, whose author is Henry Herbert Pembroke. However, she did this, paradoxically, not out of love, but of deep resentment. To publicize the homosexual love story between her husband and Michelangelo Florio was her final vengeance against them. Mary was only 16 when she married Henry, a 38 year old man, previously married twice. He died leaving his wife with less financial security than she had previously imagined.

In Henry Herbert's last will and testament there was also the odious provision that forbade Mary to remarry. However, she secretly married her doctor, Sir Matthew Lister, a much younger man. In other words, in publishing the sonnets, Mary Sidney's main desire was to publicize her husband's homosexual affair with Michelangelo Florio and shame both

of the participants, even after their deaths. Consequently, it
was of no importance to her to have a good quality product,
for its mediocrity was what she wanted and fully obtained.

XIII

FOURTH ENCODED MESSAGE
The mask of Shakespeare

In the year 1616 the actor of Stratford died, but his funeral went unobserved: it was, after all, that of an ordinary man, a simple man without merit or culture. Three years later, after Queen Anne's death, John Florio was forced to leave the Court: Unjustly deprived of his pension, he fell into poverty.

In 1620 the brothers William and Philip Pembroke, encouraged by their mother Mary Sidney, decided to finance the publication of the Florios dramas. The poetess wanted at all costs the project to be realized, so much so that she left the order in her will. John Florio was called to oversee the collection, to which he added 18 other dramas, which were still unpublished at the time. John thought that he could earn enough money to pay off some debts. The printing of the *First Folio* began in August of 1621, but stopped in October shortly after the death of Mary Sidney. The project was stalled for several months. In the meantime John was supported by the playwright and poet Ben Jonson. According to the will of Mary Sidney, which her son William would fulfill after her death, the name *Shakespeare* had to be associated with the illiterate actor. Her resentment against the Florios, first manifested with the episode related to the book *Arcadia* overseen by John in 1590, and then with the *Sonnets* of 1609, was exacerbated with the publishing of the dramas. In publishing them, the Pembrokes gained two results: the prestige to be the promoters of the initiative, and above all, the name of the Florios deleted from their own works. The Pembrokes justified this act with the idea that the book would have a better reception among readers if the plays had finally an official face and this face was English and not Italian. John, who in his lifetime had given his intellectual contribution to the various works of his contemporaries without his name ever appearing in their writings, accepted the decision of the nobles with humility and without protest. Ben Jonson, confidant of the Pembrokes, considered himself Florio's disciple, and yet he collaborated in the fraud against his own teacher.[44] He wrote, in the preface of the first edition of the *First Folio*, the eulogy for the man of Stratford on Avon, chose the poets to write verses for the dedication, and also decided that John Heminge and Henry Condell, the actor's colleagues, would appear as the editors of the dramas. The quality of the book, as it had happened with the *Sonnets*, turned out to be of inferior quality, with no care, with a bold type of mediocre ink and printed on unremarkable paper. The Pembroke brothers were more interested in satisfying the will of their mother than in the quality of the book.

On the title page of the *First Folio* there was the famous portrait by Martin Droeshout. The painter, according to tradition, had engraved the face of the man of Stratford on Avon, who had died seven years earlier, according to Heminge and Condell, doing a sort of identikit. In reality, it was done at the request of Ben Jonson, who later showed a certain perplexity concerning the literary fraud in progress and in accordance with the same Florio, an anonymous face was engraved, containing some coded messages.

One message, according to the scholar Durning-Lawrence, concerns the head drawn exaggeratedly large relative to the bust, with a visible line from the ear to the chin to indicate a real mask. In this way he wanted to represent, symbolically and once again, the contrast between the appearance and the reality, between the actor and the author. On the other hand, an engraver as famous as Droeshout could not be so incompetent as to have no sense of proportion. That things

---

[44] Florio also helped Ben Jonson in some of his works, including *Volpone*.

have gone in this way is demonstrated not only by the appreciation of Jonson for a portrait objectively unwatchable, but especially by his two sentences in the introduction of the book when referring to the actor: *Readers, look not on his picture, but his Book* and *Thou hadst small Latin and less Greek*, simple sentences to represent an indisputable truth to the point that to continue a discussion on who the real Shakespeare may be is tantamount to an offense to anyone's intelligence.

If, as Jonson writes, Shakespeare knew small Latin, how can it be possible that in his plays there are more than 500 Latin quotations? It is clear that Jonson refers to the actor, because the Florios had a vast knowledge of the Latin language.

But what escaped the observers, and what we want to highlight are the buttons on the corset of the man in the portrait. They reveal loudly, through a coded message, the name of the author of the plays. As the sum of the 30 full stops in the dedication of the *Sonnets* we have seen is equal to the sum of the letters of the names Michelangelo Florio and Henry Herbert, the sum of the **14** buttons that appear in the engraving is equivalent to the sum of the letters of the name **Giovanni Florio**.

It is a real encrypted signature. Florio's identity is also evident from the design of the button: the petals linked to the central small head symbolize the flower of Florio.

Unfortunately, even today, the mask is considered erroneously to be Shakespeare's portrait, the fictitious one, of course. In fact, people continue to ignore the real face of the man of Stratford on Avon. But if it is true, as the English say, that the actor was, in Elizabethan times, so important and well-known, why is there not a portrait of him in 1623? Of John, on the other hand, we have an incision made on the occasion of the reprint in 1611, while a portrait of him that was painted is lost.[45]

The first play at the opening of the *First Folio* is *The Tempest*, a position strongly wanted by John and significant, since it is an allegorical work on the Florios' lives and their leave from stage production.

The name of the protagonist in this play, Prospero, intended as *prosperity* is another clear hint to *florido* and *Florio* (prosperous).[46]

Even if the *First Folio* did not have the success hoped for, the Pembrokes nonetheless paid John's debts who, consequently, was very grateful to them until the end of his days.

---

[45] The Sakevilles possessesd a portrait of John Florio painted by the Dutch painter Daniel Van Mytens, portraitist of many English nobles. The existence of this portrait, which later disappeared, was aknowledged by the Earl of Dorset in 1690.

[46] See Saul Gerevini, op. cit.

XIV

FIFTH AND SIXTH ENCODED MESSAGES
The Black Stone - The School of Night

Two years after the *First Folio*'s publication, John made his will. He left his property to his second wife Rose and his daughter Aurelia.[47]   He donated to William Herbert Pembroke 340 books and a jewel called the *corvine stone*. We see a passage of the will:

> I doe likewise give and bequeat unto his noble Lordshippe the Corvine stone (as a jewel fit for a prince) which Ferdinando, the Great Duke of Tuscanie, sent as a most precious guift (among divers others) unto Queen Anna of Blessed memory, the use and vertue whereof is written in two peeces of paper both in Italian and English being in a little box with the stone.

The virtues of the stone we learn from the dictionary of the same Florio of 1598. Under Corvina is written:

> Corvia, Corvina, a stone of many vertues, found in a ravens nest, and fetcht thither by the raven, with the purpose that if in her absence a man have sodden her egs and laid them in the nest againe, she may make them raw againe.

It is a very strange definition. Meanwhile, it has to be said that, in the period we are examining, there was a lively mysticism regarding a symbolic black stone, with exceptional properties, and that the learned Arabians were trying to find that alchemic stone to give them immortality.

Certainly, the black stone which is discussed in the last will

---

[47] His first wife was also called Rose. John also lost two children during the recurring epidemics of the plague.

53

and testament is not so *miraculous* if the Grand Duke of Tuscany offers it to Queen Anne along with many other gifts, and the Queen gives it to John Florio. As Florio writes it is simply a jewel fit for a prince.

However, reading the virtues listed in the dictionary, one wonders what use a stone could have that gave back life to the crow's boiled eggs, and why someone would have boiled the eggs and then put them back in the nest.

It would seem a meaningless definition, but John seems to give much importance to the stone, beyond its economic value. Also, instead of leaving it to his beloved wife Rose, he donated it along with 340 books to the Earl of Pembroke, in a box, along with two pieces of paper on which, in Italian and English, he describes its virtues. Why? Let's try to answer these enigmas.

Firstly it has to be clarified that the definition of the stone would be absolutely without logic if in it there wasn't, as I believe, anything to decypher. *Au contraire*, it is its apparent illogicality that is the proof of what we want to sustain here.
In our opinion, on the occasion of his last will and testament Florio used the stone for delivering his last message.

Two years before the *First Folio* had been published, and the Florios dramas in it had been attributed to the illiterate actor of Stratford on Avon, Florio had accepted the Pembrokes' plot in collaboration with Ben Jonson for several reasons, especially an economic one, after having been denied a pension with the death of Queen Anne.

With the passing of months the Italian translator began to feel that that act would definitively erase the Florios' name from their dramas. This fear led him to leave once again a clue about Shakespeare's true identity. The message is given through the black stone and two pieces of paper. Let's explain our reasons. The black color of the stone recalls the black color of the *School of night* mentioned by Shakespeare in the comedy *Love's Labour's Lost*. What is that about?

The School of night was an esoteric circle whose

participants were some of the greatest minds in the Elizabethan Age, including Florio.[48] The intent of the participants was to give answers, in full freedom, to the darker aspects of existence. Later on, many members with ties to the Rosicrucians[49] and Florio himself tried to create a State in which inequality and abuse of power were banned, but giving rein to culture and free thinking, in direct contrast to the teachings of the Church, be it Catholic or Protestant. The hope of having a rosicrucian reign, expressed in some of the previous plays, but especially in *The Tempest*, was seen in the wedding of Elisabeth, daughter of James I and a student of Florio, to Prince Frederik, the Palatine Elector, celebrated in 1611. The reaction of the Papacy and the Thirty Years War put an end to the project of the political and spiritual renewal of Europe, which was supposed to begin and reside with the Court of Frederick, in Heidelberg.

In *Love's Labour's Lost* there is the personage Holofernes, identified by the English scholars as John Florio. In the play Holofernes recites the important nursery rhyme, given in the introduction of this chapter, as an example of a message in code.

Because in the comedy he is represented as a ridiculous character, for the English that would be the proof that Shakespeare and Florio are two distinct persons.

In reality, it is not so, because Shakespeare (Florio), by ridiculing Holofernes, intends to mock himself. The motive

---

[48] The school was founded by the explorer and courtier W. Raleigh and influenced by Giordano Bruno. To the school belonged also C. Marlowe, P. Sidney, E. Blount, W. Warner, R. Fludd, G. Chapman, F. Drake, T. Harriot, M. Drayton. Their association lasted 36 years, starting around 1581 until 1618, when Raleigh died.

[49] Rosacroce (Red Cross). Legendary secret order spoken about in Germany at the beginning of the 17th century, regarding the fictional adventures of a certain Christian Rosenkreuz, who lived in the 15th century, who knew all the secrets and mysterious practices of the Orient and was working on a reform for the whole world.

for which the author willingly makes himself untrustworthy has been explained as an *intentional auto-contradiction*, a technique used by different authors of the past to maintain the secrecy over determined arguments with some readers and at the same time stimulate other readers to explore further.[50] Socrates himself, under a pedagogically ridiculous cortex (bark), ordinary and clownish, would hide priceless treasures.

In other words Holofernes, with whom Shakespeare-Florio represents himself, auto-contradicting himself on purpose, talks and comports himself in such a way that for the many who are listening he is a person to laugh at, while, at the same time, a few enlightened others will understand the hidden message.

I want to point out once more that Florio lived for two years with Giordano Bruno at the French Embassy and learned a lot from his use of hermetic phrases.

That said, let's go back to the black stone and the eggs of the raven. John knew very well the expression **atanor**,[51] a term in alchemy and hermetics designating a furnace, inside which there would be deposited, and the same furnace then hermetically closed, the matter from which, after a lengthy process of mixing and remixing, you would extract the *Philosophical Stone*.

But, beware, because this procedure denotes a metaphor and describes the process that would make it possible for a normal human being to reach the best of his abilities until his transformation was complete. In other words, the matter in the egg of the *atanor* represented symbolically a new human embryo ready to be reborn; the hermetic shutting indicated the absolute isolation from the known world; the fire that would surround the melting pot was the symbol of the mental strength directed to separate the conscience of man from his

---

[50] Intentional auto-contradiction noticed by GILBERTO SACERDOTI.

[51] Term used for the first time by RAIMONDO LULLO who died in 1315. The word derives from the Hebrew *tannūt* *"Furnace"*, preceded by the article *ha-*.

animal body.

According to what we have told so far, we can deduce the first conclusions. Let's go back to the comedy *Love's Labour's Lost* and to the enigmatic phrase in which is hinted the existence of the *School of night,* for us another important encoded message:

> O paradox! Black is the badge of hell, the hue of dungeons and the School of night; And beauty's crest becomes the heavens well (4. 3).

Here Shakespeare/Florio uses the symbolism of the *atanor* to describe the characteristics and the function of the *School of night* to which he belonged. In fact, hell sends back symbolically the **flames** that heat up **the melting pot in the shape of an egg** (the secret accessible only to the followers), inside which there is the **alchemic matter** (the members of the *School of night).*

In other words, every member of the *School of night* would secretly use the fire of his mind (intelligence and culture) which would blend with the fire of the other members mind powers into a melting pot heated by the sum of all their mental powers.

The final result was the making of a new man, the *Philosopher* owner of the *true* knowledge, freed of the incrustations and errors owed to the attachments of the conscious to the animal body.

It is evident that from the free discussion and the cultural interaction among the members, dangerous concepts could surface, concepts that were contrary to the tradition and to the religious dogmas and that whoever would promulgate them could be accused of witchery and atheism, which happened to Giordano Bruno and/or to the supporters of the Copernican theory.

This was the context in which the intellectuals of the XVI century moved, and it is understood why in some anonymous plays, including those of Shakespeare/Florio (or whomever we want him to be), there existed encrypted messages that only a few could decode.

Today it's a normal fact to affirm that each individual scholar, the scientist, entering the "egg" of the scientific community must *blend* his intelligence with that of his other colleagues to the end of aquiring a greater knowledge of the world and of man, getting rid more and more of his animal component (superstitions and false beliefs).

Coming back to the jewel of Florio named in his last will and testament, let's remember that the Italian had been defined by Greene in 1593 as *upstart crow*: "crow" for his dark complexion, "upstart" because he had taken possession, according to Greene, of the works of other writers.

To Florio, as a member of the *School of night*, such nickname was probably not unwelcome, since black was the symbolic color of the school to which he belonged, and in alchemy it represented the beginning of the walk of the transmutation of man of which we have already spoken.

John Florio firstly used this nickname to launch a hermetic and personal message in his dictionary of 1598. Let's see it. It is written that the *corvine stone* has many virtues because the stone symbolizes a renewed humanity, the philosopher, with his culture and new knowledge. This stone was found in **a crow's nest and brought there by the crow**. In other words, John brought his hermetic knowledge, acquired through the exchange of "intellectual fire" with other followers of the *School of night*, inside the nest. For nest we intend his family, including Michelangelo Florio, father and his first teacher, with whom he had collaborated in the writing of anonymous dramas.

In the absence of the crow, so written, but we say in the absence of John, a man could have boiled the eggs in the water. In other words, someone could have modified or altered the dramas symbolized by the eggs. If this happened, when the eggs are placed in the nest, in other words, when the dramas are brought back to their author, it is the **crow**

John who can give them life: John can make them as they were originally.

The concern of Florio was real because in those years his plays, once delivered to the company of the *Lord Chamberlain's Men*, would undergo alterations by the actors and printers without his permission, being unable to intervene because of what we have already said. For this reason in 1598 Florio felt the need to send a message to explain his situation to the few people able to understand.

Some might find improbable what we have presented so far, objecting that the term *Corvina*, inside a dictionary with 70,000 other terms, would have gone unobserved. It is not so, because that term is strictly associated with the term *Upstart Crow* (Predatory Raven) as we saw a very important term in the field of hermetics and consequently researched by those to whom the message was directed.[52] Florio had already inserted this definition in the dictionary prior to receiving a gift from the Queen, a jewel from Tuscany, as a reward for his efforts in preparing the marriage of the princess in 1611. The Italian kept it until 1625 when he felt the need, after what had happened with the publication of the *First Folio*, to leave his last message about the true identity of Shakespeare and the production of his dramas.

To do so he used the jewel he had received as a gift from the Queen, which he called the *corvine stone* so that he could attach its meaning to the hermetic definition given in the dictionary 27 years before, which really had nothing to do with the jewel.

In his last will and testament the message was, as it has been said, for the Earl of Pembroke and his descendants

---

[52] We know from esoteric texts about alchemy what follows: if the matter in the atanor was heated fast and strongly, the operation was said to have been done in a dry way and the symbol used in the writings was **the raven**; alternatively to the dry method there was the humid method which took longer and with a slower heating temperature. In this case the animal which represented the metaphor was the toad.

because John hoped, in his naivete, that in the future they would watch over the works of the Florios, because the noble family inherited, together with 340 books, the manuscripts of the dramas.

That said, it is understandable why the Italian cared so much to put the stone in his will favoring the Pembrokes, because it was to introduce once again in a coded message the true identity of Shakespeare, a kind of testament in his testament.

He also put the jewel in a box accompanying it with not one, but two pieces of paper, one in Italian and the other in English, another symbolic element behind which we capture the truth about the production of most of the plays in two versions, Italian and English, fruit of the collaboration of two people, the Florios, father and son.

XV

SEVENTH ENCODED MESSAGE
The entry *Florio* in the Dictionary

In the Dictionary of Florio of 1598 under the letter "F" appears *Florio*, exactly like the last name of the author. It says:

> Florio is a type of bird, and between him and the **horse** there is such an **antipathy** that if the bird whistles, the horse runs away, confused.

Even this is a strange definition. In reality it is another encoded message through which the Italian translator makes us understand, at the time when the dictionary was written, the rapport between him and the actor of Stratford.

That Florio was *a type of bird* we have seen in the definition of Greene, who had defined the Italian as *crow*, an appellation that the translator had not regretted but, on the contrary, made his own for the motives already examined.

The definition continues by saying that between Florio and the horse there is *antipathy*.

If Florio is the bird, who is the horse?

In the banal events of the biography of the actor of Stratford we find that as soon as he arrived in London he was a horse attendant at a theater entrance.[53]

---

[53] So says WILLIAM DAVENANT

61

A man is often identified by his job, as it is in this case. The horse is, then, according to John Florio, the actor from Stratford.

The Italian wants to specify that even though there was a type of collaboration with the actor and financier of the company of the *Lord Chamberlain's Men* because he was the recipient of his plays, the main sentiment toward this man was antipathy. So much so that if **the bird whistles**, meaning that if Florio were to tell the truth about who the real author of the play is, the horse (the actor) *begins to run away, confused.*

XVI

EIGHTH ENCODED MESSAGE
Orige, the savage beast

Also in the *Dictionary* we find the term *Orige*, whose interpretation reveals the part which is the most shadowed and ignored in Shakespeare/Florio plays and coded messages: the great influence of Giordano Bruno on the thinking of the dramatist. It is written:

> **Orige**: a savage beast in Egypt. It looks like a goat, with the split hoofs, with a big horn on his forehead, his fur different from that of the other goats, which they say is all completely straight against Sirius when it rises, as if, by sneezing, it is adoring her.

To be able to decipher this coded message we must have a premise. As we have said, Giordano Bruno and John Florio shared a deep friendship. How many and different conversations must have occurred between the two of them! They were two Italians with vast culture, sharing the same language and philosophy of life in a foreign land. They spent hours together, I imagine in deep conversation, and, because the friar/philosopher from Nola, knowing little English, needed a translator while being in London and during the lectures he conducted at Oxford.

John was a participant at a famous dinner recounted by Bruno in *The Ash Wednesday Supper*, one of his five published works in the English city. In this book, Bruno calls himself *Teofilo* (lover of God), while John is called *messer* Florio.

In the book Bruno defends Copernicus and the heliocentric theory according to which the Earth revolves around the sun against two obtuse Aristotelian doctors of Oxford who, following tradition, affirmed the contrary.

I also want to point out that Florio appears again in another work of the Nolano with the name **Eliotropio** (sunflower).[54]

Giordano Bruno, contemptuosly and with envy defined by the Archibishop of Canterbury as the *little Italian homunculus with a name longer than his body,* was a thorn in the side of the English who would have cultural disputes with him.

By defending Copernicus, who had espoused the theory of heliocentrism against the theory of geo-centrism, Bruno understood that there was an infinite universe, without limits and many worlds, a thesis that he would develop in writings, speeches and debates in all of Europe, but which did not receive any consensus in the world of religion, science or astrology. All of this because the Roman Catholic Church wanted to defend at all costs the greco-medieval image of the world and in particular the authority of Aristotle, whose doctrines, physical, biological and philosophical, were the definition of the biblical image of the world.

To explain the rapport between God and the universe, the latter seen as a big, living being, Giordano Bruno used an example already used by Aristotle. The rapport between God and the world, he said, is the same rapport that there is between the sculptor and the statue. If I know his work, I know, to a certain extent, also the sculptor, even though not totally because the sculptor, in his statue, has only put a part of himself, and the other part stays unknown. In other words, the world is a creation of God, but that doesn't mean that God is all the world. As a philosopher, Bruno said, I can know only what God put of Himself in the world, and I can't know the whole of God, because human reason cannot go

---

[54] In *De la causa, principio et uno.*

that far.

Bruno's conception of the universe is a pantheistic one since God is everywhere, man has no privileges and he is not at the center of anything, because in the infinite there is no center and every being, be it a flea or a worm, is at the center of its world.

A philosophy that caused the Nolano to mock the occidental religions. These, according to him, had only the purpose of delineating the moral life of men, and were addressed not to the philosophers who knew good and evil, but to the ignorant and uncouth masses who needed to be governed and directed. Judaism and Christianity, according to Bruno, had separated the deity from the world and the people, banishing it to the transcendental. Because of their mistakes there was a corrupt political and social order and an impotence in front of nature. The figure of Christ was ridiculed in the work *Lo spaccio de la bestia trionfante (The expulsion of the triumphant beast)*, where the Nazarene was first identified as Orion, then as the centaur Chiron, half man and half beast. Luther and Calvin, according to the philosopher, were able to make Christianity even worse, exasperating the more negative aspects.

Bruno lauded the old Egyptian religion founded on the principle that nature is none other than God in all things and only through these natural things can you get close to Him. The gods of Egypt were human and animal and in this Bruno saw a symbolic representation of his ideas. According to him the man who looks at nature finds God and at the end he finds out that this nature-God is only he-himself. [55]

The egyptians, through intellect and imagination, had been able to cummunicate with the divinity, which Bruno saw as the Supreme Good, the first Truth, the One neo-

---

[55] It is the myth of Atteon put forward again by Bruno to explain his philosophy.

platonic, and he was convinced that the old egyptian religion was at the center of the solar religions, including Christianity.

After this premise, let's go back to the definition, a homage to Michelangelo Florio from Bruno, who at the time was imprisoned in the roman prisons and tortured by the Inquisitors. In the phrase, once again apparently senseless, there are the theses of the Nolano and his view of the wotld.

Orige, in fact, is Origene, considered one of the principal writers and theologians of the first three centuries, author of the first great system of Christian philosophy. He was an opponent of Celso, a philosopher of the II century, author of the *True Discourse*. Celso had rejected the Christian religion and also Judaism, asserting that Christianity would never find foundation in the prophecies of the Old Testament and that the idea of Christ's resurrection, manifested to only a few of his disciples, was a falsity, just as was the idea of God incarnate, because, according to him, the human race was not that superior to the bees, or elephants or ants to have this exclusive rapport with his supposed creator. The God of the Christians, according to the pagan writer, comforts the bad and pushes away those who do good. This, for him, was the height of injustice. To the contrary, the sphere of the mysterious rites deserved other consideration because it accepted in his tight circle only the pure, without fault or sins.

As we can see, the critique of Celso regarding Christianity was not very far from the one of Bruno. Florio chose Origene exactly because of his opposition against Celso.

Christianity, then, is represented by Origene (**Orige**) defined as *a savage beast,* beast because Florio wants to recall to the attention of the receivers of the message the writing of Bruno *Lo spaccio della **bestia** trionfante (The expulsion of the savage beast).* As it is known the triumphant beasts are for the philosopher, the signs of the celestial constellations, representing beasts which according to the Nolano we need to eliminate from the sky, because they represent old vices, and their time has arrived to be substituted with modern virtues: sincerity, simplicity and truth.

We need to overturn the moral concepts that have been imposed on the world, in which believing without reflecting is wisdom, human phoniness is believed to be divine advice, honor is based on wealth, and justice on tyranny.

These are concepts that Shakespeare/Florio assimilates and carried forward in his plays, in particular in the play *The Tempest*.

As we already said, according to Bruno, and, consequently to Florio, who accepts partially the conclusions of the Nolano, Christianity is responsible for the crisis in society because Saint Paul already had started the rejection of the natural values, and The Reformation did the rest. In the new order of values the first place belongs to the *truth*, after which there are other values.

So Orige (Origene) is a *beast* because it is the man who lays down the philosophical bases needed to exalt the vices condemned a long time ago by Celso and now by Bruno.

This beast is **like a goat, with the broken hoofs**, a phrase which shifts the critique of Bruno to Judaism, full of precepts useless and harmful. The goat with the broken hoofs is found in the Old Testament, where man is prohibited from eating beasts thought to be abominable, contrary to others that can be eaten without problem. In the edible foodstuff we find the goat and any beast which has **the broken hoof** divided in two nails and is a ruminant.[56]

Let's continue with the interpretation. The beast, similar to the goat, has **a big horn in the forehead**, a phrase that implies the myth of the goat Amalthea, which breast-fed Zeus. The myth says that one day, Zeus was enjoying himself

---

[56] Nonetheless in the ruminants and in those animals that have a broken hoof, you can't eat the camel, the hare, etc., because they are ruminants, even though they don't have a broken hoof, and therefore impure. The pig is also impure and even though it has a broken hoof, it is not a ruminant. Not only can you not eat the flesh of the impure beasts, but you can't even touch their cadavers (Deuteronomy 14, 3-8).

by riding the goat, holding to one of the horns so hard that he broke it. The young nymph Melissa had pity on the goat and cured the injury. Zeus, to thank her, took the broken horn, empty inside, and he gifted it to Melissa promising her that from that miraculous horn anything the owner would desire would flow. This is, of course, the horn of plenty, or the *Cornucopia*.

The why of the citation of the myth is comprehensible: Florio, just like Bruno, condemns wealth, power and the corruption generated by Judaism, represented here by the two horns of the goat, which became one. In particular, wealth has corrupted Christianity (the broken horn).

The myth also says that the goat was transformed by Zeus in a constellation and from the constellations, as we have seen, begins the criticism of Bruno in the work *The expulsion of the savage beast*.

Let's continue. The beast is in Egypt and **its fur is all straight against Sirius when it arises, as if, sneezing, he is adoring her**.

The evidence of the cult of Sirius dates back to old Egypt, a cult that through the Phoenicians arrived to the Greeks and later on the Romans. Sirius, the shining star, was often times identified with the sun.[57]

John Florio repeats the philosophy of Bruno, according to whom the origin of Christianity can go back to the *Heliolatry*, that is the adoration of the sun and to the belief that most of the old important religions of the world are connected. In other words, the beast Orige symbolizes the

---

[57] With the name **Sirius** the Greeks designated one of the stars in the southern hemisphere, whose appearance coincided with the beginning of the great summer heat. The name is already in the writings of Hesiod, used as appellation for the sun, of the planets or other stars and also, more often, to expressly designate that shining star that even nowadays is so called. On the Greek myths regarding Sirius have influenced, probably through the Phoenicians, ideas and beliefs of Egypt. The Greeks identified Sirius with Isis. In the pictorial representations of the blue horizon, the figure of Sirius is represented by the radiant crown (Encyclopedia Treccani).

Christian and Hebrew religions, whose far origins start in the cult of Sirius.

Bruno knew that Pope Leo I, in the V Century, had warned the Roman community against an open cult of the Sun, scolding those faithful christians who genuflected in front of the rising star, praying to have pity on them.[58]

Going forward with the definition we find that the fur of Orige **they tell that it stays straight against Sirius when it rises**: the Gospel says of the custom of the Pharisees to pray while standing, that is straight **(the straight fur)**, but generally the tradition of the old testament knows this type of prayer, a lyturgic ceremony that spreads also to the Christians.[59]

The act of **sneezing** by the beast shows, instead, the act of prostration of the hebrew. His prayer in front of the Western Wall (Wall of Tears) presumes, in fact, many movements of the upper body, as if he were sneezing.

Finally, **his fur contrary to the other goats**, shows how the cult of the Sun was started in Egypt by Amenofi IV and represented the first form of monotheism, Amenofi IV **contrary** to the other goats, that is, the other existing religions, all polytheistic.[60]

Florio was probably influenced by the hypothesis of the egyptian origin of the two great monotheistic faiths, Islam included. These convictions, who began from afar and were continued by the hermetic thought in the XVI century could not be expressed but in a message in code.[61] I want to remind

---

[58] In the same context in which he speaks of the **cult of the sun** (sermon 27, 3-5), Pope Leo I considers lust, greed, wrath and envy deceits of the devil and others that he calls his arts; the different expression of the magic, the divination, the spiritism, the astrology (Encyclopedia Treccani).

[59] They love to pray standing erect in the synagogue (Mt 6,5).

[60] Amenofi IV (1377-1358 b.c.), also called *Ekhnaton* (liked by Aton), imposed the adoration of one God, the solar disk Aton, starting a radical religious reform (Encyclopedia Treccani).

[61] In the translation of the *Essays* of MONTAIGNE Florio wrote: "My friend the Nolano told me, and publicly taught, that from the translation all sciences were born". In other words, philosophy, grammar, rhetoric, logic,

you that John read all the books of the Nolano to be able to compile his dictionary, in the middle of which he inserted even neapolitan terms. And furthermore, as I said, the religious questions had been fully discussed by the two Italians during the period of their common stay in the French Embassy, the same taken also to the inside of the *School of night*. Whoever professed publicly was accused of heresy, with all that it comported, which is prison and burning at the stake.

Nonetheless the Italian, as he had done in his precedent essay *Second Fruits*, wanted also to defend his friend from Nola. He did it openly at times or, as we have seen, in encryptions, according to the degree of danger of the ideas that were expressed. It was not easy for Florio, given the religious education imparted by his father Michelangelo and by the theologian Pier Paolo Vergerio, to defend Bruno. The latter one had even admitted that he had taken the Domenican habit not for a religious vocation, but to be able to study, being of humble origins.

Also Michelangelo Florio, ex-franciscan friar who later on adhered to the anti-trinity theory, believed in the existence of an only God and was convinced that man needs to be let free to direct his faith respecting his personal religiosity, sensibility and experience, without constrictions. For this, as a free spirit, Michelangelo never completely accepted the dogmatic impositions, either catholic or protestant. Having sustained the tortures in the roman prison by the Inquisitors and under the influence of the writings of the Nolano, he probably succumbed to the same fascination as his son John.[62]

---

arithmetic, geometry, astronomy, music, mathematics are sciences that come from the old Greeks, and the Greeks drew from the Egyptians, the Hebrew, the Chaldeans. It is clear that, according to Bruno, many errors were born from bad translations; in particular theologians invented the greatest absurdities.

[62] BRUNO in the *De l'infinito, universo e mondi*: "I say that the universe is

I will stop at this moment to let you know that there is no trace of a direct rapport between Bruno and the actor from Stratford. The latter one, at the time of the English sojourn of the Nolano, was a nineteen year old not yet emigrated to London. Furthermore, Bruno knew very little English and the actor never spoke another language other than his own.

Coming back to the religiosity of the Florios, it has been said that it was the influence and fascination with Bruno which the Florios incorporated into their plays. Nonetheless, the Florios never repudiated Christianity *in toto.*

After all we have said, we can understand why Bruno called Florio *Heliotrope*[63] (sunflower), a name that recalls, ironically and good-naturedly, the far origin of the Christian religion in which the translator was educated and which, as we saw, began with the egyptians and their adoration of the Star Sirius or of the sun. In other words, Bruno wanted to remind the translator that, being a Christian, by adoring Jesus you adore the sun, just like it seems that the sunflower does when it constantly revolves toward the light of the sun. Florio, as an answer, just as friendly, inserted the world vision of Bruno in the dictionary through the name Orige and chose to put on his own coat of arms the sunflower.

And yet, the Florios chose to continue practicing Christianity and, anyway, they could do no less because religion was a very big part of their cultural baggage. What I have sustained thus far explains the strange religion that emerges from the plays of Shakespeare.

The historians nowadays think that the mind of Shakespeare/Florio is impregnated with sacred writings that

---

infinite, because he doesn't have margins, end, nor surface. So we can estimate that of the innumerable stars many are moons, so many other terrestrial globes, many other worlds similar to this one." SHAKESPEARE/FLORIO writes: "God, I could be confined in the shell of a nut, and feel king of the infinite space, if I didn't have bad dreams." (Hamlet, 2,2).

[63] Eliotropio o Elitropio from the Greek heliotropion: that turns (from the verb trépein) toward the sun (helios).

emerge, maybe even without awareness, from the texts of the plays as if the author was studying professionally every day and looking at the sacred texts of the Gospel, as Michelangelo Florio had.[64] The Bible, as in the writings of the Florios, appears not so much and not only as religious text, but as a mine of words, of images, ideas, all in all as an immense literary source.[65]

---

[64] See PIERO BOITANI *The Gospel according to Shakespeare,* Mulino Editor, Bologna, 2009

[65] The actor from Stratford had a knowledge of the Bible just as any inhabitant of the land. As a young boy, to the contrary of what the English historians say, he could not have been exposed to the reading of the Bible because nobody in his house knew how to read or write. Moreover, even if he could have participated in two masses per day, night and day, for years, he could not have obtained that biblical culture found in the plays, because the lyturgic material used in those times did not include so many of the texts found in the dramas or that clearly were the inspiration. (see L. TASSINARI, op. cit. pag. 238).

XVII

THE 340 BOOKS OF THE FLORIOS

We have arrived to the end of our journey. When John Florio died two years after his works in the *First Folio* were organized, it was the beginning of the road that has taken us to what we have defined as the greatest literary fraud in history. In those years England was beginning to emerge as a European powerhouse, and it needed a great author, a cultural symbol that obviously could not be Italian.

In the ensuing years, as we have seen, gradually many documents and written testimonies that would have aknowledged the Florios the true authors of the dramas were systematically hidden or destroyed. Moreover, the British modified in the legal documents and the parochial registries the name of the actor from Stratford (for example, in the wedding registry) to coincide with the artistic name *Shakespeare* of the two Italians. Where the manumission was not possible, a complete obscurity was employed.

The Florios never imagined while they were still alive the success that their theatrical plays would have had with the passage of time. Michelangelo, even though he had a true passion for the theater, was strongly opposed to the representation of the dramas, while John decided to gain great fame through his important dictionary.

All the intellectuals and aristocrats close to John Florio, like his brother-in-law Samuel Daniel, the Pembroke family, the Earl of Southampton, the editor Thomas Thorpe, the Court, and the members of the *School of night* went along with his will to maintain the anonymity regarding his own theatrical plays.

When these people whom I mentioned, one after the other, died, the literary and theatrical fortunes of the Florios were gradually obliterated by the oblivion of time. In his writings Ben Jonson, who, while freeing himself of any moral scruple when becoming an accomplice in the fraud against the Florios, had decided to exalt himself and England in the artistic and literary field, when he assured the paternity of the plays of the two Italians to that illiterate actor.

To this first English nationalization of Shakespeare there follows a long period that begins from the re-opening of the theaters in 1660 after the plague until around 1730, during which the plays were little produced and often redone according to the taste of the Restoration.

It was around the middle of the 1700s that the myth of Shakespeare took off, thanks to the London actor David Garrick who organized a series of performances, concerts and evening galas in the occasion of the centenary of the birth of the man from Stratford.

The unstoppable success of the plays necessitated the research of biographical material on their author. Because the name of the actor did not appear in any document of the period in which he lived, the official biographers invented biographies full of gaps and unsustainable "facts".

The name Florio came back to light in 1890 when it was published, as we saw, in the ninth edition of the *Encyclopaedia Britannica*.

At that point, the Pembrokes, who had received in heredity the vast library of the Florios, thought to re-launch the myth of Shakespeare (obviously excluding the Florios), through a colossal commercial operation based on Stratford-on-Avon. They acquired houses in which the actor had lived, furnished them with effects and knick-knacks of the time, putting plaques here and there, celebrating this man born in that town, and in doing so thusly began the transformation of a little town and humble abode of the birth place of the actor Shakespeare (not the Florios, the real authors) into a shrine, a museum in order to exalt him and the epic age in which he lived.

Today the Pembrokes continue to impede the historians access to the Florios library, to the books, as it was written in the last will and testament of John, *italian, french, spanish, printed and not printed, in the number of about three hundred forty.* For what motive? Possibly because we could find manuscripts of the plays of the Florios or because some of them could have marginalia which could identify the Florios as Shakespeare.

So as not to create problems for the British national pride, but especially for commercial lucre, the Pembrokes have decided to negate the existence of the whole library. And to think that John, in his naivete, put his trust into their forefathers, as he did in Ben Jonson, when writing his will and probably hoping that maybe, in the future, they would tell the world the truth about him that he himself could never tell, given the times!

Now, I can surmise that a crazy ancestor of the Pembrokes burned 340 books to hide the Italian nationality of Shakespeare, but if the books are conserved in old trunks the Pembrokes would stain their reputation in front of humanity and especially God.

Nowadays Stratford is the most visited place in the United Kingdom. If the identity of the Bard were to be changed, the economy of the place would fall and it would probably be a bad blow to the economy in London, and let's not forget the shame in losing such a celebrated national icon.

XVIII

IGNORE AND CONFOUND

I imagine that in the readers of this work there will be a great skepticism. This is understandable. A repeated lie for four centuries cannot but become "truth" and to demolish it now appears to be an impossible task. Nevertheless, in the history of men there have been unimaginable changes.

The *question Shakespeare* looks a little like the famous *Donation of Constantine*, a document, as it is known, that established the supremacy of the Papacy over the empire and different concessions to the Church of Rome. In 1440, the Italian humanist Lorenzo Valla demonstrated unequivocally that the donation was a fake. He did this through an historic and linguistic study of the document that put into evidence anacronisms, contradictions of content and form, banal errors. But it has taken six centuries to accept the truth.

Even with Shakespeare we find contradictions and banalities if to that name we associate the actor from Stratford. It is a real paradoxical situation, the one that has been created. Who like me affirms the Italian identity of the playright giving very simple truths and with disarming evidence (and more profound studies don't do anything else but confirm what I have so far sustained) is accused of promulgating absurd fantasies. And yet all the great stratfordian biographers, nobody excluded, who have invented of new cloth the life of an actor without culture and sensibility to give credit to the idea that it was he who wrote immortal dramas, have the trust of the entire world.

After the publication of the book *Shakespeare is Italian*, an English professor that has taught for years in an Italian university, to the question of a journalist of a newspaper regarding the hypothesis that behind the name Shakespeare there are the Florios, answered: *"This theory is full of variants because there are too many Florios. There is Michelangelo and his son John, then there is Giovanni with a son; then there is another John who was a known literary person at the time and was part of the circle of the Earl of Southhampton ...."*

This professor has seminars every year on Shakespeare, and I don't doubt that he knows well, for having read them, the plays of the playright. But on the argument regarding the Florios the professor has demonstrated a discouraging ignorance, because he names three authors with the name of Florio, while in reality he is talking, without knowing, about the same person. Even If he had made a mistake, in good faith, it is not admissible that a serious scholar gives a public answer without knowing the argument.

In so doing, he has demonstated his ignorance on the studies of the authors I have mentioned, in particular those, unassailable and accredited of his countrywoman Frances Amelia Yeats who wrote, as we have seen, a biography of John Florio. The answer of the professor is an example of how the stratfordians evade any confrontation that puts in discussion their idol from Stratford.

In the face of criticism based on documental proof, because the English scholars don't have good answers, they put into action the strategy that sees two things: **ignore** and **confound**. They ignore a document or an unwelcome opinion, as long as possible. When they are obliged to respond they do so with flimsy arguments to confuse the ideas of the readers or listeners who are not familiar with the problems concerning Shakespeare.

In four centuries, the lie about Shakespeare has become a dogma into which many generations of scholars have been indoctrinated, and to question their truth means to doubt their certainties.

I hope the Italians understand my message. Wasn't the

Italian Dante the greatest teacher of coded messages in history?

O ye that have healthy intellect/ Look at the doctrine that is hidden/ Under the veil of the strange verses.[66]

---

[66] DANTE, The Divine Comedy, Inferno IX, 61-63

FINAL THOUGHTS

Many geniuses were born into humble and ignorant families. But we know all about them, because they were known to their contemporaries, and many writings of the times speak of them. Of Shakespeare we know nothing and as I have said in this essay, his biography, built by the Stratfordians, is based on "It might have been", "It probably was", "Everything points out to ... but ....". If we speak about geniuses, there are certainly lots of them who say that the author of such immortal dramas cannot be the actor of Stratford upon Avon, including Mark Twain, Henry James, Charles Dickens, and Sigmund Freud, etc. etc.

And who can forget the famous 1987 mock trial held by 3 Justices of the US Supreme Court regarding the authorship of Shakespeare's plays? Justice John Stevens was one of those 3 Justices, and 22 years later, in 2009, Justice Stevens concluded that the evidence was beyond a reasonable doubt that the Bard of Avon was NOT the author of Shakespeare's plays. Also in 2009 another US Supreme Court Justice, Justice Ruth Bader Ginsburg, recommended research into the candidate, John Florio.

My intent, in writing this book, was not to report on the very serious and profound studies of historians of international fame (such as Diana Price), who think as I do, for then I would have written an encyclopedia, but without any new facts. As I said in my metaphor at the beginning of this book, my aim has been to go directly to the heart of the problem, go back to the *Big Bang*, that is, the publication of the *First Folio*, when the biggest literary fraud ever created in the history of great frauds was put in motion.

My book is purposely short, a pamphlet, an essay which reveals a subject never mentioned before: the coded messages. Encoded messages were widely in use during Elizabethan times, for example in the hermetic writings of Giordano Bruno.

Of course, for some, the coded messages I decode may be only a fruit of my imagination, but whoever reads the book attentively should admit that the interpretation of such messages is part of a coherent and logical reconstruction of the events, where pieces of the puzzle have been put back in their right place after the British blew it up 400 years ago.

The *question Shakespeare* should have been resolved long ago if there hadn't been (and still is) the obstructionism of the powerful lobbies, State financed and sanctified by the Universities of the British kingdom. Everything revolves around the money, because on the name and entity of Shakespeare there are millions that go to the English treasury, and let's not forget the pride of the Nation which I have already mentioned in this book.

If we stipulate that Shakespeare is not the one born in Stratford, then I must conclude that regarding the Italian identity of the Bard all that happened during the 1500s and 1600s in the literary world takes us directly and easily to the Florios.

There are two last wills and testament, a simple one from the actor from Stratford, written by a lawyer, and the other, written personally by John Florio, in which he wills 340 books, an incredibly vast library for the times, which unfortunately have been lost in the years since, to the Pembrokes. The content alone in these two last wills and testaments really emphasizes the different caliber of the education of these two men, a chasm that separates the real Shakespeare (Florio) from the Stratfordian one.

Since I don't want to repeat myself, I will only point out the following: regarding the *First Folio*, Ben Jonson says that Shakespeare did not know Greek or Latin. This assertion always put the Stratfordians in a bind because, to the contrary, they affirmed and continue to do so, that in these two languages Shakespeare was incredibly proficient. Today we know (and my own paper has added another proof by decoding the messages found on the portrait to the *First*

Folio), Ben Jonson was talking about the illiterate actor and not about the real author of the plays, John Florio.

Recent studies prove that Shakespeare knew more than 25,000 words which he learned from the different languages, including Greek and Latin. Some of the texts or phrases, from which Shakespeare took inspiration for his plays, he read in the original language. That is he read French, Spanish, Italian, German, Latin, Greek, even Hebrew and more significantly, he read books in the original Tuscan and Neapolitan dialects. John Florio knew these languages extremely well (and the actor?). John Florio knew very well *The Divine Comedy* (and the actor?). John Florio translated Montaigne from French into English (and the actor?). John Florio was a contributor to different writings of different contemporary authors and translated into English Boccaccio's *Decameron* (and the actor?).

Shakespeare writes 15 plays set in Italy and he even knows, for example, a particular expression used only in Messina, or how to move from one point to another with the ferry in Venice, or the names of Italian personages almost unknown to everyday Italian inhabitants, and all of this from a guy who never left Stratford or London?

A genius can never be such unless his qualities develop with the everyday reading of many books, for years and years, books that the village of Stratford had never seen or possessed (no internet at the time and books were very expensive for regular folks).

Let's imagine this young man of 26 who arrives in London from this poor village, who is so cultured and yet has never set foot out of his village or the island. The English, not knowing how to explain this conundrum, say that all that the actor knew he learned from the Italian merchants in the taverns. Really? How ridiculous!

Besides knowing so many languages, Shakespeare had a profound knowledge of astronomy, geography, cartography, history, religion, philosophy, medicine, physics, chemistry, botany, customs and traditions of different nations, nautical art, military art, fencing, economy, jurisprudence, meteorology, diplomacy, culinary arts, proverbs, games, music, classical works, mythology, etiquette, behavior in the aristocratic world, Italian culture cryptography, legends, the occult sciences, physiognomy, etc., etc.

Who could have such profound knowledge in so many subjects? Only that Italian courtier who was a known encyclopedic scholar and intellectual, a tutor to nobles and friend of queens, a man thirsty for knowledge, who sought it constantly and had deepened such knowledge in so many different fields, especially because he needed it all to compile a dictionary with 170,000 words, and thus ... it is John Florio.

Another interesting addendum to my thesis is the fact that Shakespeare (Florio) never mentions Stratford in his plays because it was NOT his place of birth.

Regarding the name Shakespeare, we only have six signatures (as the graphologists describe) that show that the writer was illiterate. The signature, shaky and tremulous, is at times *Willm Shakp*, at others *Willim Shakspere*, or *Shaxper* etc. It is so because the ignorant actor was appropriating the *nom de plume* of the Florios.

Today the English have perfected an invented genealogical tree in which there is a father, a grandfather .... But this tree, manufactured and built on the artistic name of the Florios fraudulently tries to give credence to the myth that these ignorant peasants of Stratford were the ancestors of one of the greatest geniuses of all time. And, unfortunately, this lie, the mother of all lies and completely preposterous, is believed by the world at large.

Finally, in conclusion, I want to remind my readers and other scholars that in this essay I have deciphered 8 messages in code, 3 of which were found in *A world of words*. I am sure that John left many more disseminated in his dictionary and it is my fervent wish that other scholars, together with me, can soon find them and decipher them. It is a great challenge, but I hope that this endeavor will finally put an end to the *Question Shakespeare*.

Finito di stampare nel mese di Aprile 2016
per conto di Youcanprint *Self - Publishing*